W9-AVG-031

FOR ALL YOUR LIFE

His arms drew her to him, warm, gentle and strong.

He pressed his cheek against hers. "Anne," he whispered, "I love you very much. I think I've been in love with you for two years. Could you—"

For a moment the sweetness of it was more than Anne could bear. Then she remembered her terrible discovery: it will destroy Griff's career if he marries me.

Griff leaned over and kissed her on the mouth.

Anne's hands pressed against him. "No, Griff. No, let me go! Please!"

Bantam Books by Emilie Loring
Ask your bookseller for the books you have missed

  ACROSS THE YEARS
  FOLLOW YOUR HEART
  FOR ALL YOUR LIFE
  GIVE ME ONE SUMMER
  HOW CAN THE HEART FORGET
  RAINBOW AT DUSK
  SWIFT WATER
  WHEN HEARTS ARE LIGHT AGAIN
  WHERE BEAUTY DWELLS

EMILIE LORING
FOR ALL YOUR LIFE

BANTAM BOOKS · TORONTO · NEW YORK · LONDON

*This low-priced Bantam Book
has been completely reset in a type face
designed for easy reading, and was printed
from new plates. It contains the complete
text of the original hard-cover edition.*
NOT ONE WORD HAS BEEN OMITTED.

FOR ALL YOUR LIFE
*A Bantam Book / published by arrangement with
Little, Brown and Company*

PRINTING HISTORY
Little, Brown edition published October 1952
2nd printing .. December 1952   3rd printing ...... January 1953
Grosset & Dunlap edition published November 1953
2nd printing .... February 1954   3rd printing .. December 1954
4th printing .... November 1955
Bantam edition / June 1957

2nd printing ...... March 1960	11th printing .... April 1967
3rd printing .... April 1963	12th printing .... March 1968
4th printing .... June 1964	13th printing .... May 1968
5th printing .... June 1964	14th printing .... July 1969
6th printing .... June 1964	15th printing ...... August 1969
7th printing .. November 1964	16th printing .. December 1969
8th printing .... April 1965	17th printing .. December 1971
9th printing ...... August 1965	18th printing .... March 1977
10th printing .. December 1966	19th printing ...... March 1980

All rights reserved.
Copyright 1952 by Little, Brown and Company.

*This book may not be reproduced in whole or in part, by
mimeograph or any other means, without permission.
For information address: Little, Brown and Company,
34 Beacon Street, Boston, Massachusetts 02106.*

ISBN 0-553-13450-7

Published simultaneously in the United States and Canada

*Bantam Books are published by Bantam Books, Inc. Its trade-
mark, consisting of the words "Bantam Books" and the por-
trayal of a bantam, is Registered in U.S. Patent and Trademark
Office and in other countries. Marca Registrada. Bantam
Books, Inc., 666 Fifth Avenue, New York, New York 10019.*

PRINTED IN THE UNITED STATES OF AMERICA

From North to South, from East to West they came: the letters you wrote me when *To Love and to Honor* was published. Wonderful letters, full of commendation, affection and good wishes. I would have liked to answer each one but it would have taken weeks, and you all asked for another story. I couldn't do both, so I am dedicating *For All Your Life* to each one of you in appreciation of your generous and warm-hearted encouragement.

EMILIE LORING

All the characters and incidents in this story are imaginary and have no relation to any real persons or situations. If the name of any real person has been used it is purely coincidental and without the author's knowledge.

I

THERE WAS an outsize gold-and-crimson maple leaf of weatherproof metal attached to the trunk of a gigantic oak. Its tip pointed east. TO THE MOUNTAIN, it directed.

The girl at the wheel of the open cream-color convertible took the curve indicated at reckless speed. Since she had entered the wood road she had imagined she was being followed. Perhaps it wasn't imagination. Perhaps she had heard the muffled sound of tires on a dirt road which stopped when she stopped to listen.

She jammed on the brake with a force that sent the car to the side of the road, barely escaping a crash with the left front wheel of an open truck laden with ladders and foresters' tools. She straightened it out of a skid. Stopped. Jumped out and ran back to confront the dark-haired man in plaid shirt and navy-blue dungarees. The eyes that met hers looked enormous and coal-black in a face drained now of natural color.

"What do you mean by leaving your truck in the middle of the road where it could be hit?" she demanded breathlessly. Fright and excitement choked her. She swallowed hard. "I might have killed you. I—" a sob caught in her throat— "I hate stupid people."

His eyes traveled from the black suède cloche crushed down on her blond hair, to her beige topcoat, lingered for an instant on the outsize alligator bag which swung from her shoulder, and returned to her face.

"More likely to have killed yourself," he retorted. "Don't the roads have two sides in the part of the country you hail from? Don't people blow horns before taking curves on high? If you'll use your eyes you'll see that the truck is well on its own side of the road."

The scorn in his voice, the realization that she had been entirely in the wrong, sent a warm surge of color to her face, changed the blue-gray eyes to amethyst. Brilliant red letters on the side of the truck proclaimed to a more or less interested world that it belonged to the State Park Department.

"That's telling her!"

The voice came from above.

She looked up quickly. On the center rung of a ladder, resting against a tall maple, a man perched precariously. He was in his mid-twenties, perhaps, in a shirt and dungarees like those of the older, taller man near the truck. His grin widened

1

as he lighted a cigarette and prepared to watch the development of the battle below.

The girl firmly squelched the urge to make a gamin face at him and turned to the one whose rubber-gloved hands were busy at the truck. He wasn't bronzed enough to be an outdoor man. Nice types, both of them, she decided, and relaxed.

"I'm sorry. It was entirely my fault," she admitted handsomely. "I was determined to make the mountain before dark. Someone was—" Better not say she thought she was being followed. It sounded like imagination run wild. "These woods are scary when the sun goes down. I'm Anne Kendrick."

With an incredulous whistle and acrobatic ease, the man on the ladder slid to the ground. His hair was brick-red, his fair skin was brilliantly burned, his small eyes were hazel-green.

"Come to take possession of your legacy," he finished for her. "Welcome, by—" His cordial greeting was checked by a look from the man who was taking a crimson leaf from the pile in the truck. He corrected quickly—"By the Park Department. There's your mountain." He pointed toward the vista at the end of the road.

Dark and rugged against the deep blue of a late afternoon sky, the granite cap of the mountain loomed above the tops of low, encircling hills. Far off on the horizon the Presidential Range had donned the purple robes of early evening. A crimson sun dropped from behind an island of white cloud to spotlight a rambling stone house which appeared to be clinging to the mountainside. Its windows were now sheets of red gold.

"Is that Mountain Lodge? My house?" the girl demanded breathlessly.

"If you are Anne Kendrick, it is," the older man, still busy at the truck, confirmed. "If you intend to make it before dark you'd better start. Joe, go with Miss Kendrick. It would be a blotch on—the Park Department record—if she were lost in these hills. I'll pick you up at the Lodge. Make it fast."

"Okay, boss." The younger man grabbed a gray sweater from the seat of the truck. "Come on, Miss Kendrick. From here it looks as though you could reach out and touch your property, but it's a long way to that thar mountain." As she hesitated, he asked, "Not afraid to go with me, are you? I assure you that the boss and I had to furnish recommendations before we landed this job as emergency help. My name is Joe Bennet and the boss is—"

"Don't stop for station identification, Joseph," the older man interrupted, "or you won't reach the mountain before it is too dark for her to see the beauty of the property, with its gardens, tennis court, and the landing field visible from the game-room window."

2

"I will be glad for an escort," the girl admitted, "but I'll be taking your helper and—"

"I can spare him." For the first time since she had made her dramatic entrance into his life, the man's fine, strong face lighted in a smile. "You're wasting my time as well as the daylight," he reminded her. "I have a dozen more of these gaudy leaves to adjust."

He swung to the seat of the truck and motioned to her to go ahead. Anne slipped under the wheel of the convertible. Joe Bennet took the seat beside her.

Came the warning sound of an automobile horn.

"Hi! Griff! Griff!"

The hail and a cream-color open roadster came slowly around the curve at the same moment. A more cautious approach than her own had been, Anne admitted. The dark-haired girl at the wheel stopped the car abruptly. She flashed a glance at Anne and her companion before she concentrated on the tall man, who jumped from the truck and crossed the road to her.

"Oh, here you are, darling." She leaned from the roadster and adjusted a point of his collar. "I called at Forest Edge and Rissa told me you were laboring for the public good here. Come for bridge at nine tonight, will you, darling?"

"Yes. Beat it, Zoe. You're holding up my work."

She looked in the direction of the convertible and raised already sufficiently arched black eyebrows.

"Looks like *interesting* work, Griff."

Anne's face burned.

Why, she wondered, was she sitting here listening to a conversation not intended for her.

"Let's go," she said.

"Make it snappy," Bennet advised, "but not dangerous. I'm looking forward to a long and glamorous life." After a moment's pause he added casually, "Griff will be furious."

"Why? Because we were present at the sentimental interlude?"

"No. Because there was a sentimental interlude. Zoe Mason just won't give up—"

Anne made no comment. She realized that the truck was following and looked back. The roadster had made a U turn and was disappearing round the curve in the road.

"Don't bother about Griff," Bennet advised. "He has more leaves to adjust, as he told you. Motorists will begin to flock to see the foliage tomorrow. The different shapes and colors of these metal leaves are guides to locate the varieties. Crimson indicates sweet gum and red maple. Purple: mountain ash. Clear yellow: American beech and willow."

"Imagine knowing so much about everyday leaves. I calls

3

it pretty nice of the Park Department to make it easy for foliage hunters to locate the different trees. Isn't the first week in September a bit early for them?"

"Not this year. Turn right. We cross a small bridge, then on to the real mountain road. Thanks be, you are getting back your color. Your face was ghastly as you scraped by the truck. Warm enough?"

"Toasty. What air! What glorious air!" She drew a deep breath. "It's positively heady with the zing and fragrance of firs. I begin to feel little shivers of excitement prickling along my veins." She was aware of his quick look at her.

"Miss Kendrick, you're not setting out on this legacy-acquiring adventure alone, I hope."

"I am. Why not?"

"Because," he said bluntly, "there may be danger in it. Hasn't Cosgrove told you?"

"I haven't even seen him. How did you know he was my lawyer? You seem to know a great deal about me."

"Everyone up here knows about you. It's the great story of the year. And Cosgrove was Mrs. Williams's lawyer so I took for granted he'd be handling your new estate. But he should have warned you. Queer things have been going on at Mountain Lodge since Mrs. Williams's sudden death."

"What things?"

"For one, a cache of ten thousand dollars in hundred-dollar bills vanished from the house. Mrs. Williams drew it from the bank the morning before she died. It wasn't accounted for and hasn't been found. News of it got around." His pleasant face was troubled. "You have a father and mother, I understand. Why didn't they come with you?"

Why explain that the "mother" was a stepmother, kind but indifferent, that the "father" was a man she had married shortly after John Kendrick's death? It was too complicated.

"Don't look so surprised that I'm posted," Bennet went on. "Your coming has been our chief news for days. Residents of the county, permanent and temporary guests at the two hotels, are agog to see the girl the eccentric Mayme Williams left her fortune and estate to because she had once loved the girl's father, John Kendrick the actor."

"But there was another will," Anne reminded him. "A later will. Mr. Cosgrove saw it."

Bennet shrugged. "What does it matter? Anyhow it's missing."

"Go on and tell me," Anne invited. "Something else worries you."

"It's Mayme Williams's missing parrot," he said. "Half the community has joined in the treasure hunt for the talking

4

African parrot, Socrates by name, known as Old Soc, that was Mrs. Williams's favorite companion."

"But why steal a parrot?" Anne was bewildered.

"There is a possibility that he may repeat something said —about the missing will or the lost money."

"Mr. Cosgrove wrote me that the court had allowed the signed will in my favor and ordered him to administer the estate according to its provisions, and here I am. Listen!"

She let the engine die. "Isn't that a hermit thrush bursting its lovely throat to welcome me?"

The atmosphere was so clear the mountain seemed almost reachable by an outstretched hand. Hardwoods that showed tiny spouts of scarlet clothed its base. For a thousand feet above, spiked evergreens took over, with spruce and firs growing from spongy carpets of brown needles that were in turn replaced by low-growing shrubs and stunted trees straggling upward to the peak. The occasional mirror-glint of a quietly running brook was visible. The rambling stone house looked as though it had sprung from the land.

She sat motionless for a moment after the enchanting notes trailed off into a hushed trill. In the western sky Venus and the moon, a thin, sliver of light, were putting on a show.

"That song makes the fighting in Korea seem millions of light-years away. I'll take it as a good omen."

Bennet was watching her face, which had grown sober.

"Don't let the mystery of the place get you, Miss Kendrick. I didn't mean to frighten you."

"You haven't frightened me," she assured him quickly. "I'm just puzzled. Why did Mrs. Williams leave her estate to a girl she had never seen? Isn't there someone who has a right to claim it? Were there no blood relatives? Usually when a rich eccentric dies, cousins spring up like mushrooms."

"Not in this case. Cosgrove followed each clue till it vanished in thin air. Naturally he wanted to get the estate settled," Bennet added dryly, "so he could collect the legacy Mrs. Williams willed him."

Anne glanced at him quickly. It was abundantly evident from his voice that he did not like the man under discussion.

"What has Mr. Cosgrove done to you?" she inquired.

The question deepened his already brilliant color.

"He's opposing my best friend's return to Congress."

"What's the matter with that? Isn't it the natural procedure? I saw a statement only yesterday that one third of the Senate and all four hundred and thirty-five seats of the House are at stake this autumn. I thought healthy opposition was the food on which our nation waxed big and strong."

'Healthy, you've said it, but Cosgrove doesn't play fair.

Anyhow, we need more men like Griffith Trent in Congress. But watch your step with Cosgrove, that's all. He's tricky in his relations with human beings. Remember that. I'm afraid you'll find this a lonely place in winter."

It took her a second to follow his quick change of subject. She laughed.

"That comes under the head of an occupational hazard. It will suit me for a while. I came not only to claim my bequest but to get away from everything." Memory of the man she had come to escape heightened the color in her face.

Joe Bennet indulged in a soft whistle.

"So that's the answer. *Cherchez l'homme.*"

"It is not. If you had been notified you'd been bequeathed an estate with a handsome income attached," she added breathlessly, "wouldn't you have followed it up?"

"Followed it up? I would have flown an F-86 Saber jet to collect the prize, not taken my time in a convertible."

"Perhaps it would have been better to fly," she thought aloud.

"What do you mean by that cryptic remark?"

"I think someone followed me in a car from the time I entered the mountain region." Somehow it did not seem so silly now. She told of hearing tires on the dirt road, which stopped when she stopped.

"Know of anyone who would resent my occupation of Mountain Lodge?" she asked, trying to speak lightly.

"Why didn't you tell my pal about this?"

"I figured nine chances out of ten it was my imagination."

"Probably it was." Joe Bennet tried to sound convincing but the worried look was back on his face.

Anne drove slowly between ornate iron gates.

"What a massive, formidable front door. Something about it sets the butterfly wings in my stomach fanning."

"Don't let it get you. Do you see what I see coming down the front steps of your house?"

"Who are they? The grim-faced man and woman are pushovers for the couple in the famous painting, 'American Gothic.' "

"They are Amos and Harriet Dodge, butler and housekeeper respectively, who are fixtures here, a part of your bequest. Note the man's batlike ears. When they twitch, look out! The young-looking white-haired man heading the procession is your legal adviser, Gaston Cosgrove himself. He has his moments of corn. This is one of them."

"I feel like Columbus taking over in the name of Ferdinand and Isabella," Anne said a trifle shakily. "I should have a flag to plant."

II

"THIS IS a surprisingly modern room to find in a mountain lodge," Anne observed as she sat opposite Gaston Cosgrove in the dining room which opened off the gallery on the second floor. To her surprise she had found the lawyer waiting in the game room after she had changed her travel clothes for black velvet slacks and a long-sleeved white Italian silk shirt. Apparently he had assumed he was expected to remain for dinner.

The small round table at which they sat had been pushed close to the opening of a glass-enclosed porch gay with flower boxes. Beyond its windows spread a terrifying expanse of starry sky, giving her the shivery sensation of dangling in space.

Across the room a log fire leaped and blazed. It threw patterns on the light mahogany walls and set figures dancing in shadowy corners. The small, elegantly appointed table was an island of color and light. Yellow candes, that matched the chair seat and the long straight hangings at either side of the entrance door, burned in the tall crystal candelabra of the Adam period, flanked by two hold-leaves containing bunches of large purple grapes. Monogrammed yellow damask napkins matched in color the border of the place plates.

Anne glanced at the man in the light-gray tweeds across the table. In spite of the slightly bulging eyeballs, he was good-looking, but there was no warmth about him. He seemed cold and detached. In the early forties, perhaps, she thought. "He's tricky in his relations with human beings," Joe Bennet had warned her. Certainly he did not seem the sort of person to whom she would turn for advice in time of trouble.

In the porch window she could see the reflection of her white shirt, and like the old woman in Mother Goose, for the hundredth time since leaving home she wondered, "Can this be really I?"

"I wondered when I would rate your attention," he said as her eyes met his.

"I was trying to get accustomed to all this."

"Of course. Mayme Williams had intended to modernize the whole house; she did have the hall done but she wasn't given the time to complete the job. Too bad. I like this room. Do you?"

"Immensely. The absence of things is restful; from what

I have seen, most of the house is packed with them. Forgive my inattention, but you must admit I have reason to be dazed by the *Arabian Nights* situation in which I find myself."

"Don't you care for wine?" he asked in surprise as she raised her hand between her glass and the decanter Dodge was wielding.

"Not tonight."

"You have inherited a choice cellar."

"Which will be appreciated by my guests, doubtless. Tell me something of this property which has fallen into my lap from a clear blue sky. I don't mean the money. I will come to your office for that. I mean human-interest bits. Did Mrs. Williams make this a year-round home?"

"She married a widower, you know, who willed her the real estate. While he lived, they used the place as a summer retreat. After Williams died, his wife made it a year-round residence. I think she loved every inch of it."

"As one approaches the house it seems to have been dug out of the side of the mountain, but from inside I figured it must be at least half a mile away."

"A mile."

Anne was thoughtful. "Did all the money belong originally to Mr. Williams?"

"No, only the real estate. His money was left to his only son by a former marriage. Mrs. Williams did not need it as she had a large fortune in her own right. The money she has left to you was her own."

"Wasn't there any logical heir?"

"Logical," Cosgrove said dryly. "Not legal. Williams's son. He was the sole beneficiary of a will I drew for Mrs. Williams but it has disappeared."

"Then this place belongs rightfully to Mayme Williams's stepson. What difference does it make that the will has disappeared?"

"The difference," Cosgrove pointed out, "between his getting the estate and you getting it in a court of law. It has been assumed that after the will was drawn she destroyed it. It can't be found. The will naming you as beneficiary was discovered in her deposit box. Anyhow, the boy died in a plane that went down in the Pacific after World War II. That fact was definitely established months ago."

"And he left no heirs?"

"No."

"Tough for him. Why didn't you write me these facts?"

It took Cosgrove through courses of perfectly cooked tenderloin filets with mushrooms, a watercress and endive salad and a frozen dessert to explain.

"Coffee will be served in the game room as usual." It wasn't a question. It was a declaration of intention by Dodge standing behind her chair.

That butler appears so firmly established in the driver's seat, I wonder if I will ever get the courage to pick up the reins of this establishment and say where I want coffee served? Anne thought, as she entered the game room, which also opened off the gallery. Not an attractive spot. Antlers in several shapes and varieties decorated the walls. A collection of guns was arranged above the fireplace, where great logs were putting on a pyrotechnic show of red and orange flames. She stopped at the door of an enclosed porch identical with that which opened off the dining room.

"That looks like a large feeding box for birds outside," she said.

"It is. Mrs. Williams sat on that porch for hours at a time watching them. They came in great varieties. She kept a daily record of the number and species that fed there. You'll notice the open door of the parrot's cage to the right of the fireplace. The night Mrs. Williams died that cage was found open and Socrates was gone." Cosgrove looked around him. "Hideous room, isn't it? Of course, you are free to banish any or all of the furnishings as soon as you like."

"I'll live in the house before I make changes," Anne decided. "One has only to look from any window to see enough beauty and grandeur to make one forget the interior. Cream? Sugar?" She seated herself at the low table and picked up the antique silver coffeepot.

"Black." He lighted a cigarette and sank into a deep armchair supported on the legs of a deer. "How did you happen to run into Joe Bennet?" he asked unexpectedly.

"Joe Bennet?" Anne repeated the name, puzzled. Then her face cleared. "Oh, you mean the man who was in my car when I arrived. I met him on the road. It was getting dark and he offered to conduct me through the woods. I was fortunate to meet him and another member of the Park Department, or I might be roaming those roads now."

Cosgrove ran a hand through his white hair and laughed. "Park Department! They were kidding you. Joe Bennet is secretary to Griffith Trent, the present representative in Congress from this part of the state. He was probably the other man. Trent is breaking his neck to be re-elected. Park Department! That's the joke of the month."

"Mr. Bennet did say that he and his friend were emergency help."

"Emergency is the word. Trent and his sister own one of the old places here; his land adjoins yours. His is one of the

9

big mill families whose business has survived the ups and downs of the last hundred years. Often flies from Washington for week ends. When Congress adjourns in a few days he'll be on hand to round up his constituents. I recall now, he is a director of the Park Department."

Remembering Joe Bennet's reference to Cosgrove's bitterness toward Trent, Anne hastened to change the subject. She watched the expression of the lawyer's face as she moved to a deep chair across the hearth from him.

"I hope there is some idle cash for me to use, Mr. Cosgrove."

That stiffened him. He set down with a thud the Spode coffee cup he had raised to his lips.

"I don't want to spend it in riotous living," she explained. "I want to invest it."

He relaxed.

"I was afraid you might be in debt. Mrs. Williams wouldn't have liked that. I think it only fair to warn you that taxes will be increased for you high-bracket people. The expense of carrying this house is enormous; perhaps you can better that. To answer your question, there is an accumulation of cash which is yours to use as you like. I had thought you would modernize this house, if you intend to make it your home."

It seemed to Anne that the question implicit in his words had an insistent quality. But she was not ready to commit herself yet.

"Perhaps," she said casually, "I will lose my heart to the house as it is. I attended a class last winter organized to teach women to take care of money. It was confusing at first but as we went on my interest and, I trust, my perception, grew."

"Well, you can leave most of that to your advisers." Cosgrove was silent for a moment, ruminating. "You were directing a television program when I located you, weren't you?"

Anne nodded. "I had had some experience before, of course, as head of the Dramatic Society at college. And, as you know, my father was an actor. I had been singing on the radio when the chance came to work up the television project. I took it. I found that world as fascinating as the world of finance."

"Come to my office at eleven tomorrow and we'll go into the financial part of your bequest. There are also some pearls and other jewels at the bank to be turned over to you." Cosgrove rose. "I must go. I have a political committee waiting for me."

"Are you in politics too?" Anne asked politely, as though Joe Bennet had not told her.

"I'm running for Congress from this district."

"But isn't Mr. Trent already there?"

10

"Not permanently, I hope," Cosgrove said. "Although he has influential backing that's hard to compete with. His sister is working for him tooth and nail."

"No wife?"

"No. Griffith Trent is a woman-hater. The girl he was engaged to jilted him while he was in the service and married another man. Now that he's dead, she has come back." His grin reminded her of the Cheshire cat. "I'll let you in on a secret, Miss Kendrick. Trent was a great favorite with Mrs. Williams and she tried to make him promise to marry you."

That shocked her to her feet.

"Marry *me!*" she repeated incredulously. "*Tried* to make him promise! And he refused?"

"Absolutely. I was present when she made the proposition. Trent has been keen to have a ski lift on her—on your— mountain. *Pro bono publico* idea. He argued that it would bring winter business to the farmers, who could use more money. She refused, saying she wouldn't have this house turned into a broken-bone clinic. I backed her up. Finally she flared: 'Wait till I'm gone, Griffith, marry the girl who inherits and then you can do what you like with my mountain.' Trent was furious. He said, 'Thanks, I'm not that public-spirited.'"

Seeing the red color blazing in her cheeks, Cosgrove laughed.

"Don't let it get you down. Mayme Williams was always trying to manage other lives. Be sure and call me if there is something I can do to help. I'm still your legal adviser, you know, until you fire me." He laughed, as though the suggestion were not even a remote possibility. "Good night."

She tried to answer but anger had her by the throat. So Mrs. Williams had offered her as a wife to Griffith Trent, and he had refused: "Thanks, I'm not that public-spirited." That explained why he had been so annoyed with her when she had appeared on the road. Was the girl in the roadster the one who had turned him down? She had called him "darling."

Slowly the anger faded away. So Griffith Trent was not public-spirited enough to marry her. A mischievous smile lighted her face. I'll make him like me, she thought, and then I'll give him a brush-off he'll remember the rest of his life. Always supposing I *can* make him like me.

She glanced at her wrist watch. Eight o'clock! She held it to her ear. It had not stopped. What would she do with the rest of the evening? A maid had unpacked in the room Dodge had assigned to her. The butler at the wheel again. Very much at the wheel.

Anne crossed to the game room, now rosy dusk from the light of the red embers in the fireplace, and opened a window in the glass-enclosed porch. The crisp air stung her face.

What glory! Stars hung on the tips of branches like Christmas-tree ornaments, perched on hilltops, shot across the sky like a child skimming along an icy slide.

"You, Oh Wonderful You."

A man's impassioned singing drifted through the open window from a radio in one of the cottages of her estate. Her throat tightened; her eyes stung. A wave of homesickness submerged her. Why had she come? Why had she left the world she knew and loved for this wilderness? Of what use was money and a big estate if one wasn't in a congenial atmosphere?

As if in sympathy with her mood, from below rose a high-pitched quavering scream that sank into thin exhaustion. She closed the window quickly.

"Don't let that wail get under your skin, Miss Kendrick," advised a laughing voice. "It was just a screech owl."

It was the man who had been in charge of the Park Department truck, Griffith Trent, the man who had turned her down as a wife. He had changed from working regalia to a Gordon tartan dinner jacket which accentuated his tall leanness. She contrasted his present smiling friendliness with his curt reproof at her carelessness.

"I thought you had a date this evening," she said, and immediately regretted that she had let him know she remembered the girl in the roadster.

He took a step toward her and said, his voice low, no laughter in it now, "I had to find out who you suspected had been following you before you almost ran down the Park Department. It's important."

III

"HOW DID you know?"

Anger and resentment forgotten in surprise, Anne stepped into the game room. He closed the porch door and followed.

"How did I know? Thereby hangs a tale."

"Apparently this room is used as a living room," Anne said. "There isn't another on this floor. You probably know better than I." Hearing the sound of her voice, Anne warned herself: Watch your step or you'll antagonize him for keeps and wreck your scheme.

Griffith Trent smiled. "I ought to know it. I spent most of my boyhood summers next door. Jimmy Williams and I played Indians in these woods. After exterminating and neatly scalp-

ing the enemy we would repair to this house or mine for eats."
He poked the smoldering logs and sent a geyser of red sparks
up the chimney.

"Sit down," Anne said, "and tell me about Jimmy Williams."
This time she remembered to give him her most radiant smile
as she sank into the deep chair. Griffith Trent took the one
Gaston Cosgrove had occupied.

"Mind if I smoke?" He offered an open cigarette case.
"Will you?"

She shook her head in answer to both questions. "No, and
no thank you. Now please tell me all you know about Jimmy
Williams."

He looked very much at ease, she thought indignantly, very
much at home. They might have been sitting like this, side by
side in front of an open fire, for years.

"If I were to tell you all I know about Jimmy," he said,
"the story would have that of the Ancient Mariner licked to
a fare-thee-well. You couldn't take it. Ask me questions about
him and I'll do my best to answer."

Anne looked at him directly, and the impact of his eyes was
like an electric shock. "Do you believe he went down in a
plane over the Pacific?"

"Certainly," he said in a tone that left no doubt. "During
the war Jimmy and I were in the same outfit for four years.
I came out because I felt I could be of more use to my state
elsewhere. He stayed in the Air Force. The record of his
crash is vouched for. Why are you worried about it?"

"I'm not worried. But I want to be sure. There have been
so many mistakes in reports about missing men. I hoped this
one was wrong and that he might appear to claim his inheritance."

"But even if he did appear, he wouldn't have an inheritance," Griffith Trent told her. "He was not Mayme Williams's
legal heir. She willed this place and all the rest of her estate,
real and personal, to you, after profound consideration. The
court allowed that will."

"You don't think I'd let that prevent me from turning it
over to him if he returned, do you?"

When he smiled Griffith Trent's strong face had a warmth
that had been missing from Gaston Cosgrove's.

"You won't have a chance. Jimmy is gone."

"Was his body recovered?" Anne persisted.

"No."

"Was Mrs. Williams fond of him?"

"In a way," he answered cautiously.

"I wondered. Sometimes stepmothers—" Anne's voice trailed
off. She did not want to tell the story of her life.

"Mayme Williams was a practical person," Trent explained. "She had a strong sense of the responsibility that should go with ownership. Her stepson, Jimmy, was a dreamer and a spendthrift. His father left him a small fortune and he ran through it in no time. He would have done the same with this. Qualities like that exasperated her. I have seen no women—and one meets a lot of superintelligent women in Washington—and few men who had her grasp of business and financial details. That is why it seems incredible that ten thousand dollars in cash should be missing from this house. Mayme Williams was not the kind of person to mislay things."

He frowned at the fire as though the crumbling red embers were a television screen on which memory was staging an act.

After a pause that had no awkwardness in it, an easy, companionable pause during which they each pursued their own thoughts, Griffith went on thoughtfully, "Jimmy hadn't one business cell in his brain, if that is where such cells are located. He was a poet. Mayme Williams was proud when a volume of his verse was published, though I doubt that she ever opened the autographed copy he gave her. I never knew her to read anything but the *Congressional Record* and slathers of business and financial papers and magazines. The radio supplied the news."

"Did you read his poems?" Anne asked.

"Sure. I like poetry when it rhymes and shimmers, and Jimmy's sings too. But we've wandered a long way from the object of my call."

"Then you didn't come to see whether by any chance I were a fake claimant?" Oh, dear, she thought, I'll never make him like me if I sound as sarcastic as that.

"I knew who you were when you shot around that curve," he told her. "I had a horrible vision of a crash that would be the end of you in this world." He cleared his voice of huskiness. "But let's forget that. Let's get back to the reason for my being here tonight." There was a little pause and he added, "One reason, at least. Do you remember, while you were in the road after the near collision you said, 'Someone was—' and then you stopped? I think you intended to say—'following me.' Is that right?"

"J. Edgar Hoover, as I'm alive."

He did not answer her laughing tone. "You had been frightened," he said steadily. "Why not admit it? That is why you were traveling so fast." He added unexpectedly, "You were right."

"Right?"

"Someone was following you. Later I backtracked over the route you had covered and found the marks of tires, ground

14

deep into the growth at the side of the road, as though a car had been stopped suddenly."

Anne did not answer but she felt as though a cold hand had touched her spine. Although the room was warm she shivered.

"Look here," he said abruptly, "I don't like the way things look. You've come here a stranger, the beneficiary of an eccentric woman who didn't pull her punches if she disliked or distrusted a person. She made many enemies. They might—become your enemies."

"But—"

"You owe it to the community to report the slightest threat or annoyance. If you don't care for yourself, others might become involved in danger."

Danger? Anne thought. All at once Mountain Lodge seemed very far from her familiar world. Panic swept over her and she was ashamed of it.

"Are you the community?" she asked with a touch of mockery in her voice.

"A responsible unit of it," Griffith said soberly. "You can't divert me from my purpose by jibes and wisecracks." He added sharply, "Did you tell Gaston Cosgrove you suspected you had been followed part of the way?"

"No. Why should I?"

"How long had you been followed?"

She thought back. "The sound of tires began after I left the last town. I had stopped there in a drugstore to ask the way to the mountain."

"When you were in the drugstore did you say who you were?"

She shook her head.

"Who told you how to get here? Who was there at the time?"

"Each of three men standing with the person I figured was the proprietor eagerly offered information in reply to my questions."

"Remember their faces?"

"Yes. I was making my entrance to a region in which I expected to take up residence so I was interested to know the types of persons who would be my neighbors. One short, roly-poly man had two front teeth missing and lisped."

"Dunn." Trent drew a notebook from his pocket and wrote the name. "Go on."

"An intense, dark-haired individual with a Phi Beta Kappa key on the end of his watch chain—he kept swinging it all the time."

"Parson Savage." He entered the name in his book. "There was another?"

15

"Yes. I thought the third was of Polish extraction. He was a lot more practical than the others, told me how many miles I was from the base of the mountain and advised me to get a move on if I wanted to reach it before dark."

He added a name to the page.

"And the man you figured was the proprietor?"

"Said nothing, let the others talk. But I'd wager my convertible that if I were wanted by the FBI he could describe accurately every detail of my costume with a few extra licks for my shoulder bag."

"Tim Marston. 'The photographic eye,' he's called here. He's a power for good in this town. His pharmacy is a safe rallying place for the high-school students. A boy or girl who can show a monthly report with no mark lower than a B may order any kind of ice cream on the house every day for a week. There has been an amazing upsurge of B marks since he began the custom!"

"He must be a fine person."

Griffith Trent smiled. "You've given an unmistakable description of each man. Nice going. And incidentally, you've met the four trustees of Mayme Williams's estate. She selected them for different qualities—and wisely. You'll like them."

He poked the fire again. "You have come into a region of magnificent dairy farms located in the valley in the lap of the mountain; of people of many diverse racial strains who table their differences and work together for the good of the state. The majority of them, that is; there are some wildcatters," he qualified.

Anne wondered if he were thinking of Gaston Cosgrove's fight for his seat in Congress.

"Do you remember seeing anyone else in the drugstore?"

"Only the girl who made hot chocolate for me. She was all eyes and flutter. Her head was covered with tight, black curls. A dent in her right cheek looked like a permanent dimple. When she wasn't serving me she was giggling with someone behind the screen."

"Did you see who it was?"

Anne's eyes opened in surprise at the sharpness of the question.

"No, but her self-conscious giggle suggested a man. As soon as I finished, I followed the advice of my Polish neighbor and got a move on. A dark-green convertible, heavily monogrammed, was at the curb when I arrived and still there when I left. I didn't see another person until I almost ran you down."

"I wasn't the person in danger." He rose and stood in front of the fire, looking down at her. "You don't like me, do you?"

16

She tried to express guileless surprise but her lashes dropped when her eyes met his. The remembrance of Cosgrove's story of Mayme Williams's offer of her legatee to the man looking down at her crisped her voice.

"Are girls in the habit of registering a rise in temperature when they meet you for the first time?"

He had a wonderful laugh. Understanding was in it and tenderness, and beneath all, the force of an unconquerable spirit.

"I shall fare forth wondering if I rate your scorn." The smile vanished from his eyes and mouth. "Will you let me know if there is even a suspicion that you are being followed again?"

"Why should the burden of my safety be dropped on the shoulders of a man who hasn't seen me before today?" she protested.

"Your mistake," he told her. "I have seen you a great many times during the last two years. Mrs. Williams listened to your radio program every night and then she wanted to know what you were like. I've seen you at work. Dancing. In your investment class. And—"

"Why?"

"Scouting," he said.

She was silent. So he had seen her when he so furiously refused to marry her.

"To find out what you're like," he said. "Whether you were a proper person to inherit Mayme Williams's property. She couldn't do it herself. But we have been close friends for years. Right or wrong, she relied on my judgment of character. She backed me for Congress, you know."

"Was Mr. Cosgrove also employed as a scout?"

"He knew nothing of her plan. You and she and I are the only ones who know I was chosen to investigate for her. This is a confidence, understand? Mrs. Williams did not want Cosgrove to know there was an observer working for her."

Anne nodded. "I suppose," she said, "if you had turned thumbs down on Anne Kendrick, she would be back in New York at this moment, running a television program."

"I doubt it. Aunt Mayme—not my aunt, of course, but my sister and I have always called her that—set her heart on having the daughter of John Kendrick inherit her property. She must have loved your father very much. But she wanted to be sure you would be worthy of the trust because an estate of this size is a great responsibility."

"As though I needed to be reminded," she retored indignantly. "I haven't slept through one night since I was notified that the property had been left to me. And by a woman I'd

17

never heard of. You assumed a lot of responsibility for me. Marvelous perception, I calls it."

"No use trying to antagonize me, Miss Kendrick. Aunt Mayme deputized me to be your friend and adviser. She was afraid there might be too many problems for you."

"How absurd. I have looked after myself for years. She might as well have left me a hus—" Memory choked her. She swallowed the second syllable before she added hurriedly, "Apparently I owe all this wealth to you. I don't like being so indebted."

"You owe me *nothing*," he assured her firmly. "You owe it to yourself for being what you are. But for your own sake, and the safety of others, I ask you again to let me know if you are disturbed in any way."

This time Anne met his eyes. "I promise," she said soberly.

"Good," he said briskly. "My sister, Clarissa, the chatelaine of our home here, Forest Edge, will call tomorrow to offer any assistance within her power. I think you will like her, but watch your step. Rissa will have you working overtime on one of her pet projects before you know it. And now I'll depart." He stopped at the door. "Perhaps Mayme Williams did leave you a husband." He laughed. "Good night. Happy dreams in your new home."

He was gone before she could reply. What had he meant by "Perhaps Mayme Williams did leave you a husband"?

She listened to the diminishing sound of his footsteps on the marble floor of the entrance hall between the Persian rugs. Now what? The hands of her watch pointed to nine o'clock. Griffith Trent would be late for his appointment with the dark-haired woman who had called him "darling." What an interminable evening. Would future nights drag like this one?

She stood in front of the dying fire, seeing pictures in the red coals: the television studio; the star she had captured for the evening being made up under protest; the warm, lighted, noisy streets; a night club where a man and girl danced together rapturously. The man's face was clear. She had met him four weeks before and had been fascinated by his charm and his apparent devotion to her. Then one morning she had been awakened by her own voice asking, "For all your life?"

She had remembered his eyes, bad eyes, faithless eyes. They could not be true to any woman for all her life. Had the dream been a warning? She would take it as such. The next evening she had told him she didn't want to see him again, that—

Here she was back on the old merry-go-round, torn be-

18

tween attraction and distrust. Perhaps because she felt too alone in this strange house.

Impatiently, she tore her thoughts from the past. Why think back? She must lock the door on yesterday. She must make good on the great responsibility Mayme Williams had entrusted to her.

These were troubled times and it would be a problem to decide where she could help most. She must live and work here as normally as possible.

She paced the floor, her habit when she was working out a problem. It helped. She stopped. Dodge was at the entrance door again.

"Miss Kendrick is not receiving this evening, sir."

There was a murmur of voices and the outer door closed.

"Dodge!" she called.

He came up the stairs, his face still.

"Who was that?"

He held out the card. Ned Crane. Ned Crane! It was as though she had summoned him here by thinking of him.

"I knew you wouldn't want to see anyone this evening," Dodge said coolly.

I don't want to see Ned Crane *ever*, Anne thought, but I can't permit you to make my decisions for me.

"After this," she said crisply, "I would prefer to decide for myself. Good night, Dodge."

She walked along the gallery and closed behind her the door of the room which Dodge had allotted to her. She knew now who had followed her through the woods. Ned Crane. She would not think of him.

I won't think of him, she repeated to herself as she got into bed and snapped off the light. She yawned. What a day. A farewell party that had lasted until three in the morning, starting on the great adventure at five. So much to think of, so much—she yawned again and fell asleep.

"Get out of here!"

She was wide-awake. Had she dreamed that harsh whisper?

"And hurry if you know what's good for you."

She lay rigid, her eyes on the star-plated sky, waiting for another word. Silence. Someone was in the room. She had not noticed whether there was a bell. She was afraid to turn on the light.

No sound. Had she dreamed that voice? Perhaps, after Griffith Trent's warning, she had imagined—

"Scram!" The low harsh command appeared to come from beside the bed.

Half expecting her hand to be seized in an icy grip, Anne sat up and snapped on the light.

A tangy breeze drifted in the open window. There was no one in the room.

"Who is it?" she demanded.

She snapped off the light and lay back, tense, listening. There was no sound.

She had imagined it. No one had been there. No one could have stood beside her bed saying, "Get out of here. And hurry if you know what's good for you. Scram." No one could have said that in a low hoarse whisper, the *s*'s hissing.

IV

THE NEXT DAY at one o'clock Anne Kendrick ran up the steps at Mountain Lodge singing, "It's a Lovely Day." Her voice rose jubilantly in spite of the fact that she had returned from Gaston Cosgrove's office with her head stuffed with figures and her heart pumping overtime from excitement.

There had been lists of Mayme Williams's stocks and bonds to check; holdings of real estate in New York and cottages in the villages near Mountain Lodge, and taxes to go over. There were mortgages galore, on some of which had been written: *Never foreclose*. The eccentric woman's charities had been many, each carefully listed with the amount she had given by month or year. There was a string of lustrous pearls, rings, brooches and bracelets in a deposit box, a trunk of family silver in the vault of the bank. A sizable account had been transferred to Anne's name by the urbane, smiling president of the institution.

"Too much. Too much for one person to control," she said softly.

As she waited for the massive outer door to be opened she turned her back on the house and looked far off to a valley of fertile fields, one golden with pumpkins. There was a white village, and a number of ponds glistened like sky-blue mirrors.

Beautiful, she thought, but almost hot. This must be Indian summer. She drew off her white blazer jacket with its gold-embroidered pocket emblem; the stitching on the Peter Pan collar of her white silk blouse matched that on her flannel skirt.

She could see many roads tied together by crossroads, and wondered whether they led to the colonial farmhouses with spirals of violet smoke rising from their chimneys, and the long red barns, white-steepled churches and elm-shaded streets through which she had driven. Sunshine flooded the world. It sparkled. The sense of unbearable responsibility which had rested on her since her arrival vanished. Even the startling voice of the night before faded into part of a nightmare.

"I will lift up mine eyes to the hills, from whence cometh my help," she said under her breath and felt the spread of the wings of her spirit. She filled her lungs with the mountain air. "Who's afraid of what?" she declared dramatically. "Responsibility, here I come."

Dodge opened the door. "Did you speak to me, Miss?"

"No, Dodge. I was giving the girl who lives here a shot of courage." He looked mystified as she passed him and entered the hall. And what a hall, her thoughts trooped on, as she placed her books on a beautifully carved black teakwood table. The walls were of varicolored marble, with many wavy streaks of soft pink which gave off a rosy light. An exquisitely wrought iron balustrade, black as the teakwood, at one side of broad marble stairs, mounted to the gallery on the second floor from which doors opened.

Opposite the stairs, between two high mahogany doors, was an aquarium which covered the space from ceiling to floor and from door to door. Green aquatic plants filled the lower part and above, among the large leaves, flashed fish—yellow, pink, scarlet and red-gold. The hall was beautiful in itself but as inappropriate to a mountain lodge as a spangled frock on a dishwasher.

"It's a magnificent hall, Miss Kendrick," Dodge declared aggressively, as though he sensed her critical appraisal.

"It is, Dodge. I can't wait to give a party to see lovely girls and women sweeping up and down these marble stairs. What is behind those three closed doors across the hall on this floor?"

"They lead to the entertaining suite, Miss Kendrick. Ballroom, powder and dining room. There is a coatroom for gentlemen beyond. Mrs. Williams intended to redecorate them to harmonize with the hall but she wasn't given time."

"Did she entertain much?"

"Yes, Miss, she gave beautiful parties in her day. The house staff hopes you will do the same."

"Time will tell."

As she started toward the stairs, Dodge said, "There are two messages for you."

She stopped on the third step and looked down into his stern, seamed face, which even the rosy light from the marble wall did not soften. His large ears quivered.

"The gentleman who called last evening came again. And Miss Clarissa telephoned. Mr. Griff's sister. She asked if you would care to see her at four this afternoon. I told her you would. I will serve tea in the enclosed porch."

Dodge was not only in the driving seat. He was taking over the whole car.

He saw something of her thought in her face. "Miss Clarissa Trent is a power in this state. She is a very important person, Miss Kendrick." The butler saw that his highhanded behavior had not been forgiven.

"Mrs. Williams was very fond of Miss Clarissa. She's always lived here. She never married. She was planning to be, even her wedding dress was in the Washington house—her father was our senator at the time—but something happened and the engagement was broken. The next summer when she came home to Forest Edge her hair was white as snow."

Strange, Anne thought, that both brother and sister should have been disappointed in love.

Dodge seemed to relish an opportunity to gossip. "No one here ever saw the man; he never came up to Forest Edge. We never even knew his name. Of course, it's mostly forgotten now. It happened over four years ago."

Anne nodded and ran up the stairs. She stopped at the door of the room which Adelaide, the young chambermaid, had told her was Mrs. Williams's bedroom. It was large, with a circular window on one side from which was visible the entire valley. Although the interior was depressing, the outlook was magnificent. The furniture of reddish teakwood was too big and heavy for the space. The smaller room adjoining, which had served as a combination of boudoir and office, was bright and homelike.

Anne touched a bell and the red-haired maid appeared.

"I have decided to move into these two rooms, Adelaide. I'll use the smaller for my workroom. After you've had luncheon, we'll transfer Mrs. Williams's belongings temporarily into the room I occupied last night and move my things here."

The maid's eyes were round with fright. "Have you asked Mr. Dodge if you can, Miss? He'll be terribly put out."

"Who used to occupy the room I slept in last night?"

"Mrs. Williams's nurse-companion."

As Anne tried to open a closet door the maid said, "The closet is locked, Miss. All Mrs. Williams's personal belongings were locked up when she died. One of the trustees has the key. The closet is just full of clothes. Dodge says Mrs. Williams left all her clothing to his wife. Only don't let on I told you."

In the small boudoir which she had already rechristened workroom, Anne dialed Cosgrove's number. He answered.

"Anne Kendrick speaking. I forgot to ask whether Mrs.

22

Williams left any directions about the disposal of her wardrobe."

There was a brief pause and then Cosgrove said, "Legally, everything is yours. She did mention that she wanted Mrs. Dodge to have her clothes. However, if you want them yourself, that is up to you. The key to the closet is in Mr. Dunn's hands."

"Thank you," Anne said. "Of course, I won't want them. I'll send for the key today and have the closet cleared out."

"That's very generous of you, but I know it is what Mrs. Williams would have liked. By the way, we have an excellent country club here. Will you dine and dance with me tonight?"

Anne snatched back an impulsive "No." She had come here to live. The sooner she met and knew her neighbors the better, although there were few people with whom she would not rather have spent an evening.

"It sounds like fun," she said. "At what time shall I be ready?"

"I'll call for you at seven. It's black tie for the men and as formal as they want to make it for the gals. Also it is waltz night."

A few hours later, after having moved into Mrs. Williams's rooms with the assistance of a frightened maid, Anne looked at herself in the mirror, approved the soft moss-green crepe frock, and went out to meet Clarissa Trent.

She liked what she saw. She liked Clarissa Trent's tallness, the roundness which gave no suggestion of overweight, the lilac linen frock, the short white hair, brilliant blue eyes, the deep blue of the sea when it sparkles. More than all else she liked her gracious manner.

Clarissa held out her hand. "Griff said I would fall for you," she declared, "but he didn't tell me you were a beauty."

"Could be I'm just not his type," Anne retorted gaily. "Do you like being on the porch or is it too cool for you?"

"Too cool! I still take a morning dip in the pool at the turn of the brook—your pool, by the way. The air on this porch is as mellow and fragrant as that of a glass house, with those flower boxes at each window." She selected a straight chair and sat, shoulders back, at military ease.

Anne straightened her own shoulders as she seated herself at the low table on which Dodge had set the huge silver tea tray. I certainly have come into beautiful possessions, she thought, as she noted the Lowestoft cups and saucers and the choice of silver.

"Isn't this outlook glorious?" Clarissa Trent's eyes were on the illimitable stretch of hill-enclosed valley. "We think

23

we have something to write home about at Forest Edge, but it doesn't touch this. Look! Look! Ducks! A flock bound for your lake."

"Have I a lake too?"

"You have. Airmen know it. They used to drop down and come to call on Aunt Mayme. They have stopped coming now that she has gone."

I wonder if one of the flyers took off with the gray parrot, Anne thought, and was instantly ashamed of her doubt of men she had never seen. She hastily cleared the suspicion from her mind.

"You also own a trout stream that is the envy of every homesteader within miles."

Clarissa smiled and nodded to the butler as he came in. "Dodge, I hope you've brought extra hot water. You know I can't drink your powerful brew as is."

His seamed face crinkled into his conception of a smile as he set two antique silver teapots on the tray.

"I never forget what you like, Miss Clarissa. Set it here, Della." The dictatorial tone of the last three words were in startling contrast to his reply to the guest, which had bordered on the saccharine.

Anne caught the flash of hate and resentment in the eyes of the blond parlormaid as she set down the stand with its tiers of hors d'oeuvres and one-bite cakes. I haven't seen this maid before. How many do I employ? she wondered.

"How goes the world with you, Della?" Clarissa inquired quickly. Her smile and friendliness cleared the atmosphere.

"Very well, thank you, Miss Clarissa," the maid answered.

"You needn't wait, Dodge. We will serve ourselves," Anne said.

He departed reluctantly after checking on the amount of tea in the silver pot. The parlormaid followed.

"Have I smashed a Mountain Lodge custom by dismissing him?" Anne asked when she and Clarissa Trent were alone.

"Suppose you have? This is your bailiwick now, isn't it?" Clarissa drew her chair nearer to the tea table. "Thank heaven, they've gone. Dodge is the most efficient butler out of captivity but he cramps my conversational style. That man knows everything that goes on in the county. Not that I think him a vicious gossip, but he gets around. Look at those great ears that stand straight out from his head. They remind me of bats." She helped herself to a one-bite cake with chocolate icing, and disposed of it.

"He seems to be taking rather a high hand here," Anne confessed. "I haven't seen much of his wife yet, although she looks rather like a martinet. Have they any children?"

"One daughter named Minna," Clarissa told her. "For a

while Mrs. Williams took her on here but the girl had other ideas. She drifted to New York. I suspect that the Dodges never even hear from her." Her smile, like her brother's, was warm and friendly. Fortifying, Anne thought. "Don't let him intimidate you. He is a slick butler but he could be a tough master."

"Did he intimidate Mrs. Williams?"

"*Aunt Mayme!* I forgot for a moment that you never saw her. She was in the Great Lady tradition. Not many of them left. No one got away with anything with her—except, perhaps, Gaston Cosgrove. Griff and I always felt that he managed to keep a powerful spotlight turned on Jimmy's weaknesses. Jimmy Williams, you know, her stepson."

"Did Jimmy have weaknesses?"

"Who among us hasn't?" Clarissa answered. "I'd hate to have a spotlight trained on mine."

"But why would Mr. Cosgrove want to discredit her stepson? What would he gain by it?"

"He might have thought she would make him her heir. More probably, though, he just wanted to cause trouble. I have always thought he was a congenital mischief-maker. Some humans are like that."

Anne remembered his disparaging remarks about Griffith Trent. It was the lawyer, she realized, who had prejudiced her against him by telling her the story of his refusal to marry her. Suddenly she wondered—had he told it for that very reason?

"One thing I'll have to say for Dodge," Clarissa went on. "He knew Jimmy's faults but he always covered up for him. It must have been from affection because he had nothing to gain by it. The boy never had an extra cent with which to tip him, although Aunt Mayme made him a generous allowance after he had run through his own inheritance. Money burned a hole in his pocket. You can imagine why she didn't leave her estate to him. She was generous to a fault but she did expect that every dollar she spent would bring home its share of the bacon."

"But suppose," Anne began tentatively, "suppose she did mean the money to go to him? It seems to be common knowledge that a will was drawn after the one that left the money to me."

"Then where is it?" Clarissa demanded. "Anyhow, Jimmy is dead and he left no heirs. For a time Aunt Mayme worried about the kind of girl he might marry. The kind he seemed to like—" She broke off. "Curious, this attraction of man for woman, isn't it?"

Teacup suspended, her unseeing eyes were on the valley. Anne wondered if she were reliving the romantic episode in her own life, the one that had left her, while still young and lovely, with the prematurely white hair.

Dodge appeared at the door. "Mr. Crane," he announced, and stood aside to allow the tall blond man to enter.

Clarissa Trent sprang to her feet, the violet handbag sliding to the floor.

"What—what are you doing here?" she demanded in a choked whisper.

Ned Crane's handsome face was colorless with shock. He pulled himself together with an effort.

"You, Rissa? Now what do you know about that? I didn't remember you lived up here. I came to see Miss Kendrick. I have been seeing a lot of Miss Kendrick. I want to go on seeing a lot of her." There was a hint of what-can-you-do-about-it in the declaration. "In fact, I am going to marry her."

He looked from Clarissa to Anne, stroking his slight mustache with thumb and forefinger that were none too steady.

"Anne—" Clarissa's short laugh was tinged with hysteria— "I see you know my ex-fiancé."

V

THE THREE persons within the enclosed porch, and Dodge on the threshold, were motionless as if turned to stone by the spell of a magician, but the spell had not penetrated Anne's mind. Her thoughts raced.

She remembered Dodge had said that Clarissa Trent had been ready to be married, that invitations to the ceremony and reception had been canceled, that when she returned to Forest Edge her hair was white. A moment ago this charming, poised woman had hysterically introduced Ned Crane as her ex-fiancé and Crane had announced that he was Anne's fiancé. Crane, the man who had been her shadow since she had met him four weeks ago. The situation was too improbable to be true. But was it? Was it more improbable than the fact that she was living as owner in the house of a woman she had never seen?

Clarissa seemed to be incapable of speech. Ned Crane, for all his moment of bravado, seemed to be beyond his depth. It was up to her.

"Mr. Crane has a curious sense of humor, Clarissa," she declared, quite unaware that she had used Miss Trent's first name. "He is not my fiancé." In her memory she heard Griffith Trent's laughing voice saying, "Perhaps Mayme Williams did leave you a husband."

26

Had the words flashed through her mind as a weapon with which she could smash not only Crane's complacency but her own almost irresistible response to his fascination and charm? It was worth trying.

"Apparently Mr. Crane hasn't heard that among Mrs. Williams's bequests to me was a fiancé. Romantic love seems to be out of date these days, so I intend to accept him along with the rest of the property. The estate is too big a proposition to handle alone." Her face burned but her fingers gripping the top of the chair back were icy.

"Oh, no! *No!*" Clarissa Trent's voice registered horror. In her concern for Anne, her own distress was forgotten.

"Am I too late for tea?" Griffith Trent inquired from the threshold. He stood looking from one to another, smiling and debonair in a gray sports coat and slacks.

Even Anne's icy fingers burned. Had he heard her crazy announcement? Would he think she had taken seriously his laughing statement, "Perhaps Mayme Williams did leave you a husband?"

"It's a surprise to find you here, Crane," he said easily. He drew a chair near his sister. Under the touch of his hand on her shoulder she sank back into her seat. Crane dropped onto a gaily cushioned wicker bench with a speed that suggested weakening of the knees. The situation apparently was more than he had bargained for.

Even the imperturbable Dodge was almost stuttering as he said, "I'll bring hot toast," and he scuttled out ahead of what he probably felt was a gathering storm.

Anne resumed her place at the tea table, wondering who would break the silence.

"This situation needs clarifying," Crane announced with an attempt at the light touch.

"I think it has been completely clarified," Anne countered. "You make a surprise entrance and declare yourself my fiancé. I say that you are not, that I have found a dream man more to my taste. Period."

That brought him to his feet. His fair skin was darkly red, his blue eyes narrowed in anger.

"I appealed to your taste during the more than three weeks that you dined and danced with me nightly, didn't I? You aren't going to deny that, are you, Anne?"

"I am denying nothing," she declared passionately. "But you forget that the last evening we spent together I told you I didn't want to see you again."

"If that's the way you feel about it—"

"It expresses my meaning perfectly."

"Anne, you don't mean it." There was beguiling warmth in his voice, his eyes probed hers. She could feel herself weak-

27

ening. "You can't fool me," he said. "I don't believe in this prospective fiancé. He's just a subterfuge hustled up in an emergency by your theatrical imagination. Isn't that it, Anne? Isn't it because you are afraid not of me but of yourself?"

She did not answer.

Crane turned to Griffith Trent and the warmth was gone from his voice. "You interfered in my life once before, Trent. I have you to thank for this brush-off."

"On the contrary," Griffith said coolly, "I didn't know that you and Miss Kendrick had met. If I had—"

"Don't think," Crane interrupted hastily as though to cut off something he feared was coming, "that I'll give up what I want so easily, Anne. I'll be seeing you." On that prophecy he departed.

There was silence behind him until the sound of his footsteps on the marble stairs died in the distance. Anne drew a long, unsteady breath.

"That seems to be that," she said. "How do you like your tea, Mr. Trent?"

"Strong. No trimmings. What's this about a fiancé wished on you by Mayme Williams? Are you sure that isn't something Gaston Cosgrove thought up?"

"No one," Anne said hastily, "but I, myself, is responsible for that crazy announcement. The fiancé was an emergency invention. I met Ned Crane for the first time four weeks ago. I did dine and dance with him and enjoyed being with him, but for several reasons I decided not to see him again and I told him so. Now you know the whole thing."

"I wonder if I do," Trent responded thoughtfully. "It will serve for the present. Will you go to the country club with me tonight?"

"Thanks and regrets. I have already accepted an invitation from Mr. Cosgrove. Same date. Same place."

"I'm out of luck. I'll try again," he said casually as if it made no difference to him. Why should she think it would? Hadn't he refused her as a wife? And after, she remembered, he had seen her not once but over and over, according to his own account.

"All right now, Rissa?" he inquired tenderly.

"Of course I'm all right," she retorted indignantly. "Don't speak to me as though I'd been dragged back from the jaws of death, Griff. I was just startled by the sudden appearance of Ned Crane. For a terrified instant I thought he was the ghost of the man I so nearly married." She shivered as if a memory had touched her with icy fingers, and brushed a hand across her eyes as if to dispel a haze.

Then she was once more the poised Clarissa Trent. "Anne," she said, "I would like your undivided attention. There are

28

half a dozen projects in which I am keen to interest you."

She radiated energy and sparkle. Apparently the page of life on which was written the return of Ned Crane had been turned and would remain turned.

Anne regarded her with admiration and wonder. She had loved the man enough to promise to marry him. Now it had taken her only a few minutes to recover from the shock of seeing him. She was not a fickle person so he must have hurt her deeply. It was not surprising. Anne had decided for herself that it was not in him to be true.

"I'm a pushover for any interesting project," she responded gaily in an attempt to dispel a tinge of gloom the recent episode had left. "Name your poison." She laughed. "Charge up that flippancy to the deleterious effect of TV. It's a hangover from the last Western I used on television."

Clarissa smiled. "I hope the first suggestion won't be poison. Griff and I want to give a tea to introduce you to your neighbors. It will be the first afternoon after Congress adjourns for the short autumn vacation, the exact date to be set later. Would you like it?"

"Love it," Anne assured her eagerly. "I adore festivities. Are your other propositions as glamorous as that one?"

"No. Our Red Cross needs another ambulance—there is one in your garage—and a driver to meet the casualties being returned from Korea who need to be transported from the airfield to the veterans' hospital about twenty miles beyond. Will you take over?"

"Gladly. I'd like the chance to help. I have driven for the Red Cross before. Next?"

"That's enough for now, Rissa," her brother declared. "Give Miss Kendrick time to digest those two propositions. We must go."

"Right, Griff." Clarissa Trent rose. For a moment she hesitated and the color in her face deepened. "Anne, don't let any thought of me stop you if you feel drawn to Ned Crane."

Anne shook her head. "When I told him in New York that I didn't want to see him again, it was before I knew he had touched your life in any way. Let's try to forget about him. Tell me what kind of dress to wear tonight at the club wingding."

"Not too formal. The same sort of thing you'd wear to the theater if you planned to dance later." Clarissa caught Anne's hands in hers. "It will be a joy to have you in this house. Life is going to be a heap more interesting."

"I heartily second that sentiment," Griffith Trent declared. "Come on, Rissa."

Anne accompanied them to the head of the marble stairs.

"I haven't been able to figure out," she said, "why Mrs. Williams didn't have a Persian runner on these stairs to deaden the sound when she had such a profusion of beautiful rugs everywhere else."

"She went out very little the last of her life," Griff Trent explained. "It amused her to sit in the game room and try to figure out from the sound on the stairs who was coming. She threatened to write a book on the way a footstep revealed character. Again, come on, Rissa."

Clarissa Trent started down the stairs. "This time we are really going. We'll see you this evening at the club. *Au revoir*."

Anne returned to the game room. She stood at the window where Mayme Williams had so often listened to the sound of descending feet. The tap, tap came from Clarissa's high heels. The heavier tread from her brother's sport shoes. What characteristics could one learn from—

They had stopped halfway down. Were they returning for something forgotten? Voices. Whom had they met? Not Ned Crane! She wouldn't put it past him to return. She had all she could take this afternoon. Where was Dodge?

Someone coming up. Someone who was taking the stairs two at a time. At the door of the game room she barely missed collision with Griffith Trent's red-haired secretary, Joe Bennet.

He radiated excitement; his sunburned face was crimson. He breathed fast and hard as he caught her hands and drew her back into the room.

"Quick! Before Dodge gets here." His whisper came in puffs. "Keep this under your hat. I think I've seen Mayme Williams's lost parrot."

VI

IN HER excitement Anne caught Joe Bennet's sleeve and drew him farther into the game room.

"Where, *where* did you see Mayme Williams's parrot?" she demanded.

"Hey! Calm down. I wouldn't swear it was the old bird but I think—here comes Dodge. He's on the warpath. His ears are twitching. Going to the country club tonight? Quick! I've got to beat it."

"Yes. *Yes*." She made a desperate effort to control her excitement as the butler entered.

"I've come to remove the tea tray, Miss Kendrick," he

30

announced and entered the porch. Anne walked beside Joe Bennet to the head of the stairs.

"I'm dining at the club as Mr. Cosgrove's guest," she explained in a low voice. "When will you tell me?"

"Save me the first dance after dinner." His whisper was almost inaudible. "Because—" As Dodge returned with the tea tray he switched the subject easily. "Have you seen the raffish dark-green convertible with blinding gilt monograms that's dashing around town? It belongs to a guest at the inn, a man named Crane." He drifted toward the lift at one end of the gallery, muttering *sotto voce* to Anne, "Dodge knows all. Sees all."

"He does indeed. I'm surprised that he doesn't know you have found the—" Joe's fingers lightly closed her lips.

"Remember," he said, "walls have ears. I'll bet these are hiding other things too. If the hint I gave you should leak out, someone might draw a red herring across the trail. That parrot was stolen for a purpose. I'll shove along. I have news for Griff."

"He won't lose the election, will he?" she inquired, and then wondered why she should care if he did.

"He won't be defeated," Joe said confidently. "If the industries here have to get into gear for war production, there is no man in the state better fitted for the job of telling Congress what it may count on. Hush-hush about my possible find, remember. See you tonight."

The sound of feet running down the marble stairs. The bang of the massive entrance door synchronized to the second with Dodge's return to the gallery.

"May I have a word with you, Miss Kendrick?"

Old Man Trouble coming up, she decided as she noted his grim expression and twitching ears.

"Certainly, Dodge." She entered the game room. He followed. Cleared his throat.

"I see you have moved into Mrs. Williams's rooms. You should have consulted me first."

Anger reddened Anne's cheeks. Her eyes met his squarely.

"Why should I consult you, Dodge? I am sole owner of this house and everything in it. You and your wife are here to carry out my orders, not to tell me what is to be done. The moment you presume to dictate, your usefulness is ended. You'll go."

"You can't discharge us."

She dragged her eyes from the hypnotic lure of his ears, which had developed a tendency to flap, and rigidly controlled a nervous laugh.

"You're mistaken, Dodge. Mrs. Williams provided a pension

for you and your wife in case you were not satisfactory to me or you didn't care to stay on here. It is not nearly as much as you are paid now—you'll have to admit that your present salaries are princely—but you could live on it."

"Does that mean we are fired?"

"Not at all. I like what I have seen of your work. Remember that I make decisions as to what is to be done here and I am sure we can live together in peace. Who plans the meals?"

"My wife. Why? Aren't they satisfactory?"

"Yes. I want to have a talk with her. Please ask her to come to my room tomorrow morning at ten-thirty. I shall not be at home for dinner."

"Yes, Miss Kendrick."

He bowed stiffly and departed. Angry as she had been at his presumption, she had listened carefully while he spoke. Not a hiss in a paragraph.

She turned to see Joe Bennet on the threshold. "Mayme herself couldn't have done a better job," he approved. "That's the sort of talk Dodge understands. You were calm as a summer sea. Cool as a Deepfreeze."

"Was I? I'm glad. It isn't my idea of the way to talk to persons working for me, but the Dodges need special handling. In the words of my Revolutionary ancestor, John Stark, 'Live free or die.' It was becoming apparent that I couldn't live free with Dodge dictating, and, God willing, I don't intend to die. What brought you back? I thought you had gone."

"To make sure you understood the dance you are to save for me is to be *after* dinner. You'll be swamped with partners. Dodge appeared before I could drive it in."

"You drove all right. I'll save it. Every nerve is tingling with impatience to hear the facts of your find."

"If it is a find. Don't get your hopes too high. I'm off. Keep a stiff front with Dodge and you'll be the winnah." He held his clasped hands above his head and shook them twice, prizering style, before he plummeted down the stairs.

She stood at the top and watched his rapid descent. Dodge was at the door to open it. Boy, how she had dreaded the showdown with the butler. From the first time he had served dinner—was it only last night?—she had known it was inevitable. He had appeared to take her ultimatum in his stride, but who knew what thoughts were simmering between those twitching ears? On the way to her room she remembered advice her father had given her:

"Anne, here's a rule for all your life," he had begun gravely. "When you have decided on a course of action, go to it. No matter if discouragement blocks the way, keep swinging.

Each swing will inch you forward though it may seem to you that you haven't moved. Then, before you know it, you will have achieved your goal."

Something tells me that the battle with Dodge will take a series of swings, she thought, as she closed behind her the door of the large room which had been Mayme Williams's.

She leaned against it and checked on the changes. The place began to seem homelike. The massive reddish teakwood dresser didn't look so massive with the top covered with her choicest *filet* lace runner, with crystal, silver and enameled toilet equipment and photograph frames glistening on top.

Her powder-blue brocade spread covered the bed. Her great-great-grandmother's mahogany sewing table, which she had brought in her car, stood in the curve of the circular window beside a low chair with a gay cushion from the porch, the chair in which Mayme Williams had sat when she watched the birds. She had stored most of her lares and penates until after she had seen her new house, but these familiar objects glowed in their new surroundings like the embers of a low fire and warmed her heart.

At the window she looked at the spread of the valley, rose-tinted from the afterglow. Smoke rising from many chimneys was reddish purple, headlights of automobiles flashed and shone like crimson mirrors. High in the darkening sky a lone star twinkled.

Was one of the cars the raffish dark-green convertible with blinding gold monograms that had been at the curb of the pharmacy yesterday afternoon when she had inquired the distance to the mountain? The man behind the screen, talking to the giggling girl, must have been Ned Crane. Of course he had recognized her voice. Equally of course it had been he who had followed her car along the wood road.

Looks as if I had another battle there, she told herself.

Before beginning to dress for the evening, she took a last look out of the window, peering down at the woods and wondering exactly where Forest Edge was. Not, she told herself hastily, that it mattered.

At almost the same moment, Clarissa Trent, at the door of the rambling natural-color shingled house at Forest Edge, looked back at the path through the woods she and her brother had followed from Mountain Lodge.

"Griff, I wonder how many times you and I have raced or run or walked along that path? The coloring of the leaves is more beautiful than ever this year."

"Perhaps they are celebrating the fact that someone young and lovely has come to take over Mountain Lodge," he suggested as they entered the oval, oak-paneled hall, scented by the aroma from big birch logs blazing in the fireplace at one side. In its light the large rug on the floor glowed as if jeweled. Comfortable chairs upholstered in the same green as the hangings at two French windows, invited relaxation; a table held a lamp with a bronze shade, and books gave the room a lived-in atmosphere. A spiral staircase wound its way up against a wall. Clarissa stood looking down into the flames.

"You are one hundred per cent right, Griff. Anne Kendrick is young and lovely. There is a quality in her voice, deep and warm, that sends a glow through my veins. She'll be an ideal head of that establishment," she declared. "Do —do you think Ned Crane is after *her* money?"

He rested an elbow on a corner of the carved oak mantel above the fireplace.

"The fact that she has come into a big estate doubtless carries weight with him. The story has made headlines everywhere. I wouldn't put it past Crane to decide to look her over. He came. He saw. He almost conquered. He may yet. Even without a fortune she is a mighty attractive, talented girl who would be desirable."

His sister looked at him quickly before turning back to the orange-and-scarlet flames.

"How do you know so much about her? This is only the second time you've met her."

"The third. Remember, I told you she almost ran me down in the wood road?" He laughed.

"I fell for her the moment I saw her," Clarissa said. "She's so alive. She would have suited Aunt Mayme down to the ground. It is curious she never invited the girl to come here so that she could see for herself the sort of person to whom she intended to leave her estate."

"Perhaps," Griff said lightly, "Aunt Mayme trusted to Gaston Cosgrove's report."

"No, Griff. He told me himself he never heard of Anne Kendrick until after Aunt Mayme died." She returned to her main preoccupation. "If Ned Crane has really fallen in love with her, plus her fortune, he won't give up without a fight to the finish. He has an awful lot of charm. Griff, should we tell Anne what we know about him?"

"No! No!" he said swiftly. "She already distrusts him. She must work it out for herself."

"Suppose he wins her over? Suppose she marries him? He would wreck her life."

"I doubt if anyone could wreck that girl's life. She would pick up the wreckage and build something worth-while with it."

He cleared his voice. Better soft-pedal his remarks or he would reveal the fact that he had seen Anne Kendrick at work, at play. Mayme Williams had made him promise not to reveal the fact to family or friends.

'It seems to me," Clarissa said in a worried tone, "we ought at least to hoist a danger signal."

"No! We keep hands off. Understand, Rissa?"

"Good heavens, don't roar at me, Griff. Of course I understand." More than you suspect, she added under her breath.

VII

THE MAID, in a black frock, and white cap and apron, handed Clarissa a card.

"A phone message for you, Miss Trent."

"Thank you, Ellen." She read the penciled lines twice. "Zoe Mason wants to sit with us at the club tonight, Griff. She says she is quite alone."

"I don't know why we should care if she is. Let her find someone—"

A young girl with two brown cocker spaniels at her heels broke a tempestuous descent of the stairs.

"Hi! Simon Legree is on the rampage!" she called over the banisters.

Griffith Trent looked at her above the cigarette he was lighting and laughed.

"Your Aunt Rissa just accused me of roaring at her. Sorry to sound like a slave driver. Join us, Sharon."

The girl catapulted down the rest of the stairs and landed on the rug with a swirl of forest-green wool skirt. Rough and Ready, the two dogs, who had followed, sat on their haunches, mouths open, and watched her with soft brown eyes. She was slender and willowy and pretty, each movement as graceful as those of a ballerina but unstudied. Her beige sweater and cardigan accentuated the darkness of her eyes and short hair.

"Where's the fire?" Trent inquired. "You pelted down those stairs as if a fire demon or a guilty conscience was yelping at your heels."

"Ber-lieve me, my conscience for the moment is licking its chops with contentment at my faultless behavior. The fire is here." Hand over her heart, she pirouetted across the rug and slipped her hand under his arm.

"Take me to the country club tonight, will you, Squire?"

"Ask Aunt Rissa if you may go. She's your boss."

"I did this morning. She told me to ask you. I've got to

35

go. I've made a date for dinner. Don't prick up your ears, boys. I'm not speaking of your dinner." As if in disappointment the two dogs flopped flat and rested their heads on outstretched paws.

"With whom?" the Trents demanded in unison.

Griff glanced quickly at his sister. Had she thought for a frightened second, as he had, that their niece might have met Ned Crane and made a date with him? Young as she had been during Clarissa's engagement, she had become great friends with Ned.

"Chorus by alarmed guardians. Keep your shirts on, folks." Her eyes and voice indicated that this was her idea of the ultimate in teasing. "Joe Bennet is my date. He's as safe as school and about as exciting. He treats me as if I were still in the second grade. No one believes I'm grown-up. From now on, I'm going to tell everyone I'm at least nineteen. Joe promised to meet me at the club, so you see I can't break the date, ber-lieve it or not."

"Sharon," her aunt said in exasperation, "if you say ber-lieve it or not again I shall scream."

"Okay. I'll remember, Aunt Rissa. How's the new woman at Mountain Lodge? You called there, didn't you?"

"She is charming."

"Did you see her, Uncle Griff?"

"Yes. I agree with Rissa."

"Really! My pal Janey says she bets she eats with her knife. Put a beggar on horseback motif, et cetera."

Griff recognized the provocative note in her voice. He refused the bait, smiled and shook his head.

"Miss Ames, you amaze me. It's incredible that a movie addict like you wouldn't know that the screen has been teaching table manners for years. The most underprivileged diner-out now knows which fork to pick up."

"Right in the bull's-eye, Griffy. Take me to the club, *please.*" She pressed her head against his sleeve, which was a signal for the two dogs to rise and rub against his gray slacks.

"You've given me the brush-off, dating Joe Bennet."

"Ber—believe me, only because I had a hunch you'd think it your duty to take the new woman at Mountain Lodge."

"Stop calling her 'the new woman.' She's a girl and a college graduate, you may inform your pal Janey." He knew by her grin and delighted giggle that because of his impatience she had chalked up a score for herself. He moderated his voice. "I am not taking Miss Kendrick to the club. She is to be Gaston Cosgrove's guest."

"If she's going with that stinker—"

"Sharon!"

"The family chorus again. As I was saying before so rudely

36

interrupted, that's all I want to know about her. A girl who prefers to go out with the man who is trying to snitch your place in Congress to going with you—"

"That will do, Sharon."

"I'm dumb. I recognize your stand-and-deliver voice."

"Smart gal. Your Aunt Rissa has invited another guest to sit at our table—"

"Griff," Clarissa protested, "she invited herself."

"Then I bet it's that pain in the neck—"

"Be ready at seven," her uncle interrupted. "I'll be seeing you." He picked up a bunch of letters from the table, opened a long window and stepped to the terrace. Before he closed it he heard a suppressed giggle.

"Golly, I've made him mad."

Rissa's decision to modernize the terrace had been a tremendous success, Griff acknowledged as he looked about. She had read of an Italian's artistic skill and employed him. The work had taken all summer but the finished product was worth waiting for.

A majolica-tiled floor presented in warm browns and reds and greens a view of the nearby mountain. Rush-bottom chairs looked and were comfortable. Gigantic pots of Vesuvian lava holding lemon trees in fruit flanked two rush-bottomed benches. The gaudy window blinds had been copied from Italy.

"It's all right," he approved aloud. He stopped for a moment to look at the valley high-lighted by the rosy afternoon glow. Did Anne Kendrick appreciate the glorious view from Mountain Lodge, or would even a few days of it bore her?

Give the girl time. She hadn't been in her new home much more than twenty-four hours. It was a curious coincidence that Ned Crane, the man who had come so near to being his brother-in-law, should arrive as her admirer. Thank God, Crane's presence had not affected Rissa, after the initial shock. But hang it all, why did the tragic episode of her broken engagement have to be dragged into their lives again?

He dropped into the rush chaise beside the table, poked a gay cushion behind his head and picked up his letters. If the mail he received from his constituents told a true story, his seat in Congress would be safe in the coming election. Why was John Clinton writing to him? He drew from its envelope the sheet of paper with *House of Representatives* at the top. He admired and liked the man and respected his judgment. What was on his mind now?

Trent read intently. After touching on an amusing item of scuttlebutt going the rounds of the cloakrooms, Clinton wrote:

Your seat like mine is at the mercy of the voters. Pray God we win. The new Congress will convene under the cloud of an international crisis. I think you and I have the right ideas. I'd like you in my corner. If I go back I'll have to find a new secretary. Mine has been recalled to submarine service. Warm regards to you and your sister. I still think she would be useful in Washington.

JOHN CLINTON

Eyes fixed unseeingly on violet smoke coiling upward like a serpent from a distant chimney, Trent considered the closing lines of the letter. Clinton was from the wheat country, a man of entirely different background from his own New England training. He was a man with ideas of integrity and honor and plenty of the stuff it took to get ahead. They had voted alike on many bills.

Clinton was right about Rissa, his thoughts trooped on. She was as brilliant and had a heap more political sense than many of the influential women in the capital, but since her broken engagement she had frozen at the mention of spending a winter in Washington. Possibly John Clinton could change her mind. He would invite him to come to Forest Edge the next time he came back.

Griff grinned companionably at the mountains and confided to their misting purple peaks, "At this moment a matchmaker was born."

His thoughts slid away from Rissa to Anne Kendrick. She would be superb Washington material. With opportunity and environment, she would go far. His smile vanished. Hang it all, why should the thought of Ned Crane dim his rosy picture? What had turned Anne against the man? And where had she picked up the idea of a fiancé selected by Mayme Williams?

"Hi, Griff!" Joe Bennet hailed him from an open French window. He came in waving a sheet of paper.

"Joe! It came!"

"Yeah. I'm in the Marines now."

"I'm glad because I know you wanted to go. But I'm darned sorry for myself because I'll be losing you. When did you hear?"

"Early this afternoon. I didn't stop to tell you when we met on the stairs at Mountain Lodge because I had some startling news for Miss Kendrick."

"Has the missing will be found? Or the missing ten thousand dollars?"

"Gosh, no! But I am willing to swear I saw—"

"Telephone for you, Mr. Griff," the maid announced from the doorway.

"I'm coming, thank you. Save your news until I get back,

Joe." He entered his study through one of the French windows and picked up the telephone.

"Griffith Trent speaking." He heard heavy breathing before a woman's low-pitched voice said:

"Mr. Trent, I must talk to you. I am in deep trouble. I—I am Jimmy Williams's widow."

VIII

WHEN ANNE entered the clubhouse an orchestra was playing, "Zoom Zoom. My Little Heart Goes Boom."

The gay waltz tune banished the sense of impending trouble which had haunted her since the mysterious warning of the night before, and which had been increased by the advent of Ned Crane. The atmosphere of the large old-fashioned house was heart-warming. The *décor* was modern and gay. Large vases of September garden flowers added color and fragrance.

The dining room hangings and chair covers were a beautiful cardinal red. Divans against one wall were covered in a broad white and narrow black stripe. The center of the floor was clear for dancing.

She caught her reflection in an old-time pier mirror between two windows. Her white chiffon frock with its deep V neckline and a silver lamé jacket were perfect for the occasion, and simple pearl earrings were a perfect accessory to the costume.

The women present added color to the room with their pretty dresses, and there was a sprinkling of uniforms among the black dinner jackets.

"Miss Kendrick," Cosgrove said, indicating the dining-room captain, who had seated them, "this is Leland. Miss Kendrick, the new owner of Mountain Lodge."

The man beamed approval. "Proud to see you here, Miss Kendrick. Mrs. Williams was a valued director of the club. I was always glad to see her at a meeting. She kept the temperatures of the committees down to normal when there were symptoms rising of a spending fever. She knew what the club needed to a teaspoon and what it didn't. I hope we'll see you here often."

He bowed impressively and hurried away to seat a party of five standing in the doorway.

"That's Griff Trent and his sister. I wonder why she wears violet so much, makes me think of a half-widow," Cosgrove remarked. "The dark-haired young girl with them is their orphen niece, Sharon Ames. She has made her home at Forest Edge since the death of her parents. She was very sick with flu last winter and the doctor ordered her to take a year from school. She owns one third of the Trent mill property."

"She is very pretty."

"And knows it. The other woman, the dark-haired beauty, is Mrs. Zoe Mason, who jilted Trent to marry an army captain. He died during the war. It looks as though Trent is going to try again."

Anne looked at the girl who had called to Griff on the wood road, addressing him as "darling." She had her hand on his arm and she was laughing up at him. There was no answering smile on his face. It looked drawn and tense as though he were deeply worried about something.

Cosgrove, his eyes still on the party, went on, "Joe Bennet is with them. But you've met him, of course. He is the so-called Park Department man who showed you the way to Mountain Lodge. He is from old mill stock like the Trents. Usually the entrance of that group would draw attention from every member in the room but tonight you are the center of attraction."

Anne was already aware that their table was the cynosure of many eyes.

"Is this a representative gathering of residents?" she asked. "If it is, I am completely sold on my neighbors. They look interesting."

"Except for a smattering from the two hotels, the majority are homeowners. This is an industrial state, many of the head men have homes in this valley. Mayme Williams's husband was a big shot in the mill world." Cosgrove broke off for a moment, his eyes narrowed. "Who is the tall, blond guy who just came in with the two overdressed girls?"

At that moment Ned Crane caught Anne's eyes and bowed.

"You know him, Miss Kendrick?"

Anne looked up to see the lawyer watching her curiously. She was annoyed to feel herself blushing.

"I met him in New York," she said. "His name is Crane. Tell me more about these people, Mr. Cosgrove."

Her request neatly detoured the subject of Ned Crane. Before he had time to launch into a description of her future neighbors, he was interrupted as they began to come to the table themselves, eager to meet and welcome Anne. First among them were the four trustees, who reminded her that they had seen her first, at the drugstore, and so were entitled to a dance.

During a lull, Cosgrove said, "Let's dance before any more folks come to meet you. That's a dandy tune they're playing. Know the name?"

She said she did and that she loved "Tales from the Vienna Woods" best of all the Johann Strauss waltzes. As they joined the dancers she saw Ned Crane stop at the Trent table. He bent over Clarissa. Griff Trent had risen to his feet and Anne thought, Prepare for fireworks. To her surprise, Clarissa nodded and she and Ned Crane swung into step with the music. Griff Trent resumed his seat, his eyes following the white-haired woman revolving in the arms of the tall, blond man. Beside him Zoe Mason was crumbling a roll on her plate, her heavily rouged mouth sulky.

"What startled you?" Cosgrove inquired. "You drew a long shaky breath as if you were frightened."

"I was. The hefty major who just passed stepped on my sandal. His foot is large, his dancing powerful. For one awful instant I thought my toes were crushed." It was all true if not the occasion of the breath of relief.

When they returned to their table the waitress brought broiled chicken with the customary accompaniments plus a salad of pale-green lettuce, sections of pink grapefruit and avocado with French dressing.

Cosgrove monologued on the subject of Mrs. Williams and her property. Occasionally Anne interrupted to ask a question for which there had not been an opportunity when she was at his office in the morning.

"This is a party," she apologized. "It is very wrong of me to encourage you to talk business."

"I like it," he said, "especially when questions are as intelligent as yours. Now that our state's great military base is again to hum with activity I hope to sell the two medium-size estates you own. Remember, I showed you photos of them? I hear that some brass connected with the base may want to buy—"

"May I have this dance?"

Ned Crane loomed over Anne. He was stroking his mustache with thumb and forefinger and smiling as if confident of her answer. Better to dance with him than to rouse her host's curiosity by refusing.

"Thank you, if Mr. Cosgrove will excuse me," she said. She introduced the two men.

"Did I hear you say something about selling property?" Crane asked.

"You did, indeed," Cosgrove said heartily. "Are you in the market?"

"No, but before we dance," Crane said smoothly, "I want Mr. Cosgrove to meet the young ladies I brought from the inn. Right up his street. They are looking for property here to buy."

"An exchange of partners is a fair proposition, Mr. Crane. Lead me to 'em."

When Crane returned to Anne's table he was jubilant. "There's always a way. I anticipated difficulty in getting rid of your current beau but he fairly ate out of my hand. They're playing 'Tennessee Waltz.' Let's go."

They danced to the haunting music. Crane sang softly close to her ear.

" 'My friend stole my sweetheart away.' Is that what happened, Anne?"

She made no answer. Dancing with him brought back happy evenings in New York when they had talked and laughed and danced together. He was a handsome man, he danced well, he had great charm, but—but—

As the music faded he stopped at the door of the wide porch.

"Come out. I want to talk to you."

She opened her lips to refuse but couples with the same idea had crowded behind them. Only one way to go and that's out, she decided.

"What a gorgeous night," she exclaimed as they crossed the porch to the enclosing wall. "And what sparkling air. Carbonated is the word, it's full of zip and zing." She drew a deep breath.

As Crane remained silent she went on nervously, "The sky is so clear the stars appear to be winking. An air pilot may be guiding his course by that very star at which I'm gazing; a sailor may be steering by it. Hitch your wagon to a star—it isn't bad advice, is it?" She was aware that she had been talking fast and a trifle breathlessly.

"Now that you've got the heavenly universe off your mind," Crane said, "let's return to earth and ourselves." He caught her by the elbows and swung her to the top of the wall.

"Sit there while I point out the error of your ways." His laughing eyes, his caressing voice exerted their old charm and set her wondering if he were really as faithless as she had thought him. No. She put her foot down hard on the friendly reflection. She was fast slipping under his influence again, even after the revelation of the afternoon that he had once been about to marry Clarissa Trent. There must have been a tragic reason for the break between them. Whichever way she turned, the warning posted appeared to be *prenez garde*. This time she would heed it. She was aware of Ned Crane's smile, of his blond head bent toward her. She remembered suddenly the phantom fiancé whom she had claimed. She must not forget that he believed her engaged to another man.

He was very close to her now. Suddenly Anne slid off the wall, eluded his outflung arm, and started across the porch. Halfway to the door she met Griffith Trent.

He looked from her to Ned Crane.

42

"Here you are, Miss Kendrick," he said easily. "That waltz you promised me is off to a good start."

Crane, who had followed Anne, caught him savagely by the shoulders and swung him around. Light from a long open window revealed the ugly line of Crane's mouth.

They mustn't fight, Anne thought, horrified. They mustn't fight. She tried for a light touch. "That's hammy acting," she said with a little ripple of laughter. Then she could have bitten her tongue out. Her laugh had added to Crane's fury.

"So you are the guy she thinks she has inherited, Trent." Crane's hands tightened viciously. "You can't do that to me."

"Then I'll do this."

Trent whirled swiftly, caught Crane off balance and knocked him over the wall. A crash of shrubs announced the landing of a body, and the muttering and thrashing that followed indicated that no serious injury had resulted.

Trent pulled his black dinner jacket in place on his shoulders.

"How about that waltz?" he asked as casually as if dropping a man over a porch wall were a daily exercise. "Don't let those sounds coming from among the shrubs disturb you. They are playing 'Out of a Clear Blue Sky.' Let's go."

"I ought to be able to waltz to that," Anne declared as they entered the clubhouse. "It is the way my legacy arrived." Her troubled eyes met his.

"I hope you haven't started a feud with Mr. Crane on my account." He held her closely but gently. Her steps followed his in perfect rhythm.

His laugh brought color surging back to her face. "No one can handle me like that and get away with it. Anyhow, I have another account to settle with Crane before I get to yours."

"There is no account to settle for me."

"Glad to hear it. Made to dance together, weren't we? Let's go around the room once more."

She valiantly resisted the temptation to say "Yes." His dancing was effortless, smooth as velvet. She agreed mentally that they were made to dance together. Then she remembered his words to Mrs. Williams; "I'm not that public-spirited."

"No."

He laughed. "Don't be cross about it. It was only a suggestion, not an order."

"Did I sound cross? Sorry. Usually I'm known as Sunny Anne," she said gaily.

She was angry with herself. This dance was my chance to begin my revenge by charming him, she thought. Instead, I have been cross. I never seem to find the right time to give my plan a workout.

As she sat down at Cosgrove's table the latter greeted Trent stiffly.

"Good evening, Cosgrove," Trent said pleasantly. With a laughing, "I'll be back for the rest of that waltz, Anne," he departed.

"You seem to know each other," Cosgrove said quickly.

"He called with his sister this afternoon," Anne said vaguely. "How about the young ladies? Are they going to buy the houses?"

That changed the subject and his mood as she had been sure it would. While he told her that he had made an appointment to show the girls the houses on his list she remembered that dinner was nearly over. She must save the next dance for Joe Bennet.

The music began. "Zoom, Zoom" again. Voices rose to accompany it. "My little heart went zoom. A thunderous boom."

Thank goodness, Joe Bennet was making a beeline for their table. Cosgrove watched him coming, his face set in an angry expression. Anne's pulses hummed. Apparently Cosgrove disliked Trent's secretary as much as he disliked Trent himself. Suppose he made an issue of her dancing with him? She had no choice. She had promised Joe. Anyhow, it might be her only chance to find out what had happened to the strangely missing parrot.

"Our waltz, Miss Kendrick," Joe said, smiling.

Cosgrove was on his feet. Boy, oh boy, now what? Anne asked herself. Peace or battle?

IX

TO ANNE'S surprise Cosgrove's reaction to Joe Bennet's arrival was cordial.

"Sure. Go ahead. If I bring the most attractive girl in the room I expect to pay the penalty of competition. I see Crane has deserted his dinner companions." He smiled at Anne. "While you are enjoying yourself, I'll try to sell some of your houses for you. The young ladies tell me that some of their friends are also looking for inland homes. Look after Miss Kendrick for me, Bennet."

As Anne and Bennet joined the dancers his eyes followed the lawyer's jaunty progress across the room.

"What has got into Cosgrove?" he demanded. "In all the years I have known him he has always had a grouch on

44

when he spoke to me. What started those waves of geniality radiating? It must be the influence of your sunny self."

Anne laughed. "Sunny isn't the word for me tonight somehow. I think it is the excitement of prospective sales that has him in such a twitter."

He danced her out into the lobby.

"Get your wrap from the powder room," Joe said. "That jacket is stunning but it won't be warm enough. And make it fast," he pleaded.

When he reappeared, settling a crimson muffler under the collar of his topcoat, she hummed "Fair Harvard."

A few minutes later, as they sat side by side on a bench under a mammoth oak that had not shed its leaves, she whispered, "This is remote. Communists could exchange secret papers here in absolute safety. Now why the dickens," she added in surprise, "did I think of that?" With a little shiver she snuggled deeper into her long white evening cape with its heavy gold embroidery.

"Pokey out here, I calls it. It would be dark as a pocket if it were not for the light of the stars. Why am I monologuing on the 'heavenly universe'—a quote. Begin at the beginning, Joe. Where—where did you see—it?"

"After lunch I was driving by a farm outside the town when I heard a familiar squawk—gray parrots do not scream. 'Old Soc,' I said, and my heart went boom. In my surprise I must have cut the motor, for when my brain stopped zoom-zooming I was staring at a parrot chained to a perch. There was a house beyond the white fence at the gate of which my car had stopped, and the parrot was hanging outside a window.

"While I was wondering what to do, a portly woman with short pepper-and-salt hair opened the door. I knew the place had changed owners recently and figured she was a member of the new family. 'Are you looking for someone?' she called. Her question shattered the coma that had held me spellbound. I pulled out a small notebook and approached the door."

"Why the gumshoeing to inquire about a parrot?" Anne asked.

"You forget that Mrs. Williams's bird disappeared under suspicious circumstances. 'I am looking for Mrs. John Blake,' I explained, knowing that a family named Blake had recently sold the place. 'Our selectmen want her to run for office.' Her face glowed like a harvest moon. 'Do you elect women to office in this state?' she inquired eagerly. 'I've always hoped I'd get a chance to serve on a committee.'

"I dished out some complimentary remarks—they were sincere, too; I take off my hat to a woman who wants to serve her state. Then I appeared to see the parrot for the first time. 'Quite a bird,' I said. 'Does it talk?'

" 'I don't know,' she answered. 'My husband saw it perched on the low branch of a tree on his way home last night. Picked it off like an apple. The poor thing was stiff with cold. We kept it in the kitchen last night. Jake knocked up the perch this morning and set it out in the sun.'

" 'Has it talked?' I asked.

" 'Not a word,' she said. 'I'm afraid of the creature. Its eyes looked at me as if deciding where to take a bite.' "

"Was Old Soc vicious?" Anne inquired.

"Only with Dodge. He hated that butler. I asked the woman if she would sell the bird. Told her I had a friend who was crazy to own a parrot. 'I'd give the creature away,' she came back promptly. 'I don't want it around, but my husband found it so I suppose the bird is his. If you'll drop in early tomorrow morning—our phone isn't in yet—I'll let you know if my husband will sell. I'll be tickled pink to get it off the place.'

"I departed. I dared not push for an earlier decision. I didn't take too much stock in the woman's story. It could have been a trick to find out why I wanted the bird."

"But, after all, Joe, what makes you think it is Old Soc?"

"In the first place, there aren't many gray parrots around. In the second place, here is a stray bird that no one can account for, and not far off a bird that looks just like it is missing. Just as I turned away from the door the parrot croaked, 'Smart cooky!' and followed that with Old Soc's wicked chuckle. 'Smart cooky' is new. In spite of that, I'll bet I've found the bird the reward has been offered for."

A crash of branches and the sound of a heavy fall brought them to their feet.

"There he goes! Catch him! He's been listening—"

Joe Bennet was not. He was hot in pursuit of a running figure. He returned breathless in a few moments.

"Disappeared," he panted. "One minute I saw h-him— the next he w-wasn't there. I wonder if he had pals roosting up there with him."

He stepped up on the bench. Caught a limb of the tree, swung himself into it. He brought down a shower of leaves. Nothing else.

"That was a lone scout, Joe. You'd better come down," Anne advised in a husky whisper, "or we'll have the entire club membership here to check on our sanity."

"Right." His voice was low and hoarse from exertion. "Get out from under. I'll drop."

"Who do you think was in the tree?" Anne inquired as she helped him brush dried grass from his clothing. "There—" she straightened his tie—"you begin to look like a respectable member of society. What became of your muffler?"

"Must have dropped it between the clubhouse and this tree. The person responsible for losing the parrot, I'd say, was the listening post. May have traced it to the farmhouse. May have seen me there. May have been on my track all day."

"Too many maybes. I'm sure of the person who stole Socrates originally. Dodge."

"Could be," Joe said, "but I doubt it. The parrot would have put up a terrific fight if the butler had come near his cage. You are my friend who is crazy to own the parrot. Will you be ready to fare forth with me at eight-thirty tomorrow morning?"

"At dawn, if you say the word."

"Eight-thirty will serve. Come on. We'd better get back or your legal adviser will be looking for us."

"Wait a minute, Joe. How did Socrates react to Gaston Cosgrove?"

"That guy had no reason to steal the parrot. Anyhow, they got along as easy as a couple of lovebirds."

As they approached the clubhouse she whispered, "What will you do if the parrot is gone in the morning?"

"Hunt for the guy who says 'Smart cooky.' Old Soc has learned that since he left Mountain Lodge. It wasn't in his vocabulary before."

In the lobby, after they had disposed of her cape and Bennet's topcoat, they came face to face with Griffith Trent and his niece. The girl's expression was sultry. The orchestra was repeating the "Tennessee Waltz."

"You walked out on our dance, Joe," Sharon Ames accused him and slipped a possessive hand under his arm.

"I'm sorry. I had important business to discuss with Miss Kendrick. That reminds me, two of our best friends haven't met."

Sharon nodded curtly. "Come on, Joe, or we'll miss the little that remains of this waltz."

With an apologetic glance at Anne, Bennet put his arm around Sharon and they joined the dancers.

"I apologize for my niece's rotten manners," Griff Trent declared. "I knew we had spoiled her, because she was so ill, but not to that extent. Will you finish this dance with me?" As she glanced toward her table he added, "Cosgrove is having a whale of a time with one of the girls from the Inn."

He was. Anne could see him among the dancers, with the girl's cheek pressed to his. She made a sudden decision.

"Instead of dancing could we have a minute's talk?"

"You'll need a wrap."

"It isn't cold. Let's not waste time."

In answer, he tucked her hand under his arm and led her

across the porch and down the steps. He understood her quick glance toward the shrubs and laughed.

"Don't worry about Crane. He has probably gone back to the Inn to repair the damages. Let's go for those two chairs beside the pool. We can hear the music from there."

When she was seated he touched the lamé jacket. "For warmth, this isn't worth the powder to blow it," he protested.

"We won't be here but a minute." Eyes on the pool, which was yellow-gold with star reflections as a field of dandelions, voice low, she said, "You warned me that I owed it to the community to tell you if I were threatened in any way."

"I did. I meant it."

She told him about the voice in her room the night before.

There was a pause. Then he said, "Are you sure it wasn't a nightmare? You must have been very tired after the long drive."

"Very sure."

"Then I believe I can explain how the trick was worked —though not who did it. You were in the bedroom Mrs. Williams's companion used to occupy. In the wall beside the bed there is a small grating. Did you notice it?"

She nodded.

"That communicates with a similar opening in the wall in Aunt Mayme's room. If you touch a button, a two-way communication is established between the rooms. The reason I know is because I arranged to have it done."

"I understand that part," she said in relief. "It was frightening, feeling someone was there, almost within touch, and not seeing anyone. But I still don't understand who could have done it. Why would anyone try to drive me out? Suppose I went? The house would still be mine."

Griff was silent, thinking. At last he said, "Have you spoken to anyone about this? Anyone at all?"

"No."

"That's a break. Don't. We'll keep it strictly between you and me. Do you think you could recognize it if you heard it again?"

"It was a whisper," she reminded him. "Hard to tell. I don't even know for sure whether it was a man or a woman. There was one thing—" she hesitated.

"Go on," he said encouragingly, his eyes on her face.

"The s's hissed. I know that if I heard it again, even if I couldn't recognize the voice."

"I think," he warned her, "even if you should recognize the voice, it might be wise not to show that you do."

She shivered. "You really think I am in danger, don't you?"

"You might be," he said, his voice steadying. "We'd better go back. By the way, did you notice the button beside the grating, that opening in the wall?"

"Yes."

"If you snap it and it turns red the current is on. Keep it off until I return. I'm flying to New York tomorrow. I shall stop there on my way to Washington. It may be two weeks before Congress adjourns for a vacation. Wait for me."

"Wait? For what?"

"For a solution of the case of the threatening voice," he explained lightly as they crossed the porch. "That sounds like an Erle Stanley Gardner thriller, doesn't it? We'll solve it together." He followed her through a long open window into the dining room, put his arm around her and drew her close.

"Meanwhile, why waste a note of this waltz?"

Just before they reached Cosgrove, who rose as they approached, Trent whispered, "Be careful, Anne. Be very careful."

X

"I LIKE a prompt gal," Joe Bennet declared as at exactly eight-thirty the next morning Anne stepped into his roadster.

"We have a crackajack day for the parrot hunt," he approved as the car started.

Anne drew a deep breath. "That woodsy breeze is straight from a thousand hills. See the colors on the distant mountains and the valley change as the clouds sail across the sun? Every stream and pond is a sky-blue mirror. What a beautiful world! God grant that it may be speedily at peace."

As Joe was silent she said, "Forgive me. That little prayer just burst through."

"You're not the only person who offers a prayer for peace."

She touched his hand on the wheel gently in response to his gruff reminder.

"I know I'm not, and all those prayers will help. Remember Tennyson's 'More things are wrought by prayer than this world dreams of'? I believe it. Having paid tribute to my Maker and the beauty of His world, I want you to tell me more about the parrot. Are we to buy it even if you discover that it isn't Mrs. Williams's bird?"

Joe considered. "Why not?" he said at length. "We'll put it in Socrates's cage. In some way known only to the feathered tribes, it may attract Old Soc. What will you offer for it?"

49

"Better sound out the woman first," Anne decided, "and stick to the amount of the reward that was offered by the trustees. If we offer any more, she'll get an exaggerated idea of the parrot's value."

Joe chuckled.

"Aunt Mayme's answer to the last dot of an *i*. You're one hundred per cent right. Say, there is a sting in this—quote—breeze from a thousand hills—unquote. Is that gray flannel suit warm enough?"

"I am wearing a cardigan under the jacket, see?" She pulled a bit of lemon-yellow wool above the collar.

"Matches your gloves. Snappy outfit. Hat's the same little number you wore the day you arrived, isn't it? I hope your *soigné* getup won't boost the price of the parrot."

"Say the word, brother," Anne laughed, "and I'll roll in the road and dim the gloss before we make our entrance."

"Humorous gal, aren't you, and before breakfast, too. Or are you luckier than I am?"

"No. I didn't want the Dodges to know I was going out. I left a note on the hall table that I would be back by ten-thirty. Can't we pick up a cup of coffee and a roll at the pharmacy?"

"Okay, if you can hold out until after we call for the parrot."

"Of course I can hold out. I don't like to talk about myself, but you should see and hear me sparkle after my morning coffee. Yesterday I felt doomed. This morning I'm on top of the world. In the words of Henry Van Dyke, music by Anne Kendrick—

I want a ship that's westward bound to plough the rolling
    sea,
To the Blessed Land of Room Enough beyond the ocean
    bars,
Where the air is full of sunlight and the flag is full of
    stars."

Her voice rose triumphantly on the last two lines.

Full of stars,

sang an echo among the hills.

Stars,

another answered faintly.

"If you can sing like that, Anne, my girl, what are you doing here? You ought to be singing at the Met," Joe Bennet demanded gruffly and brushed a gloved hand across his eyes.

"It was good, wasn't it?" The inquiry held a hint of panic. "I never sang like that before. Suddenly my voice wanted out. It frightened me. Something in this gorgeous day touched off a spark in my soul or heart or lungs, wherever a voice comes from. Perhaps this spicy morning air has gone to my head."

With a sudden shift of mood she went on, "Enough about me. Have you even a smidgin of a hint as to the person who was roosting in the tree above our heads when we were talking last evening?"

"No. I asked the club manager if he had heard of any hoodlums hanging round the club."

"Had he?"

"No, this is a law-abiding community as a rule. Probably it was a kid perched in the tree to watch the dancing in the dinging room. I used to do it myself when I was a kid and had a crush on a girl whom I suspected of two-timing me. Even if he overheard me, it would mean nothing to him."

"We'll hope so. This is the best time of day to motor, isn't it? Few cars on the road, and the world looking as if it had been hosed and scrubbed in the night, and this zippy air to blow the cobwebs from my brain."

"Cobwebs? A minute ago you were the original little bright-eyes."

"That was a mere figure of speech." She could not tell him that she had slept with one eye and one ear open all night, waiting for a sound that would betray someone at the other end of the grating in her wall. She had obeyed Griff Trent's orders and broken the connection between the rooms, but she had kept alert for sounds. Nothing had occurred, and toward dawn she had drifted into an uneasy sleep.

All during that wakeful night she had wondered who was trying to frighten her away. Someone who lived in the house? One of her own servants? She had no idea how many she employed, she had not seen all of them. Someone who had got in from outside? But how? And why—why—why?

Whoever it was would be pleased, she thought, to know how frightened she had been, how her heart had pounded as she lay tense and wakeful, afraid to go to sleep, listening to the sounds she had not yet learned to identify in the house. Footsteps? Whispers? Yes, someone would be very pleased indeed. But she made up her mind they should not have that pleasure. She would not betray the fact that she was alarmed. Not to anyone.

"Not going shut-eye on me now, are you? You haven't spoken for minutes," Bennet ribbed.

51

"I have a busy day ahead. I've been briefing it."

"Brief it aloud. I'd like to know what a girl like you considers a busy day."

"First, an interview with Harriet Dodge, my housekeeper. And if she is like her husband, boy, how I dread it! At ten-thirty."

"If you get home in time."

"You know, Joe," Anne went on, "since my arrival I've gone about in a daze, trying to realize what has happened to me. I must take hold of life with both hands and all my intelligence. I intend to know that house I have inherited from top to bottom and manage it just as I would a business. Mr. Cosgrove warned me that taxes would take another bite at my income. Why waste money?"

"You sound like a good business woman," Joe said.

"I'll have to be. By the way, you said this farm we're headed for isn't far beyond the village."

"It isn't. We'll be there in five minutes, but we may have to follow up the parrot."

It seemed less than five minutes later when he stopped the roadster at the gate in a white fence. Before he could step from the car a woman's voice inside the house called, "Here he is, Jake! Maybe he's brought it back."

"That has an ominous sound," Bennet declared. He was halfway up the path to the house when a big man in dungarees and a blinding tartan shirt charged toward him like an enraged bull.

"Are you the fella who come here yesterday and talked about the parrot?" The question was more a growl than a voice.

"I am. Are you Jake? I've come this morning—we've come," he corrected as Anne joined him, "to buy the parrot if you'll sell."

"You've got nerve. After stealing the critter last night."

"Keep your shirt on, Jake. Why should I be here at this time in the morning, or any time, if I had already taken the parrot?"

"You might have come back for this." Jake whipped a crimson muffler from the pocket of his dungarees.

"Well, I'll be da—darned. Where did you get that?"

"You willin' to say it's yours?"

"Sure, I'll say it's mine. Remember, Anne, I put it on when we left the clubhouse last evening?"

"Yes. Didn't I say the color fairly screamed Harvard, fair Harvard? When did you miss the parrot, Mr—"

"Our name is Wingate," supplied the round-faced woman with graying hair who had taken an aggressive stand beside her man. "Tell them what happened, Jake."

"I get up at four to milk. A few minutes before that this morning I thought I heard the kitchen floor creak. I listened so hard I dropped off in a doze. When the alarm went off I got out of bed on the jump. I went into the kitchen. Switched on the light. This here red scarf was on the floor. And no parrot."

Joe thought for a moment. "You are newcomers in the valley," he said. "Evidently you don't know that some time ago a pet parrot was stolen from that large house that looks as if it were hanging to the side of the mountain. See it?"

Husband and wife nodded.

"Miss Kendrick here and I were sitting under a tree last evening talking about the mysterious disappearance of the parrot from the big house, and the reward that's been offered for its return when—"

He told of what happened up to the time when they re-entered the clubhouse.

"It looks as though the guy in the tree must have overheard our conversation and decided that he could use the reward. So he came here and took the bird."

Jake looked at his wife. She nodded approval.

"I told you," she said, "that he seemed honest."

"Well," her husband pointed out, "that doesn't bring back the parrot or get us the reward."

Joe looked from one to another. If they were not honest then he didn't know much about people. "Look around for someone who says 'Smart cooky,'" he advised them.

"Why?"

"Because the parrot had picked up that pharse somewhere in the last few months. Find the person who uses that phrase and he or she may lead you straight to a five-hundred-dollar reward."

The man's eyes widened. "With five hundred dollars, Martha, we could—"

His wife interrupted his rosy dream. "First," she said practically, "we've got to get back the parrot. Sakes alive! My *c-a-k-e!*" she shrieked and ran toward the house as a strong smell of burning filled the air.

Her husband turned to watch her panicky departure and shook his head.

"Martha is always like that, always forgettin' an' never on time," he explained. "We've been married thirty years. I've tried to train her. No use. I like her just the same," he added with a sheepish grin.

"She looks darn likable," Joe Bennet agreed. "If you are convinced I didn't steal that parrot, we'll be shovin' along. In case you find any trace of it, get in touch with Miss Kendrick. I won't be here. I report to the Marines next week."

"Joe! Why didn't you tell me!" Anne reproached him.

Jake laid a massive hand on his shoulder. "Do you now? We've got a son with them. Perhaps you'll meet. He's Jake Wingate, Junior."

"I'll keep a lookout for him. Meanwhile, be sure you tell Miss Kendrick anything you find out about the parrot. The reward will be all yours if you return that bird to her. But keep your information hush-hush." As the woman, red-faced and breathless, rejoined her husband, he asked, "Did your cake burn, Mrs. Wingate?"

"No, I rescued it in time. Have you folks had breakfast? I'd be tickled pink to give you coffee and doughnuts and—"

"Thanks a million, Mrs. Wingate," Anne cut in hurriedly, aware of the gleam the word "doughnuts" had lighted in Joe's eyes. "We can't stay. Come on, Joe."

As the roadster moved away, Joe looked back at the man and woman standing in the middle of the front walk.

"Martha appears to be laying down the law to Jake."

"But he likes her just the same," Anne laughed.

"Do you suppose she is telling him I shouldn't be allowed to escape?"

"I think," Anne said more soberly, "she thinks that crimson muffler wasn't explained very convincingly. Someone took it deliberately, Joe, to throw suspicion on you."

"I know." He tried to shake off her worried expression. "What was the big idea of dragging me away from those doughnuts? I'll bet they are crispy brown on the outside, not palefaces like those served at the Inn."

She laughed.

"Don't beat me, Joseph. You'll feel a lot happier after you've had coffee. Curious how cross men are when hungry, even those who are happy-go-lucky at other times. I didn't know you were staying at the Inn. I had an idea you had a home here."

"The family moved to New York after I finished my freshman year at high school. They get a lot of fun out of living, Anne," he added thoughtfully. "They love their work. I'm terribly proud of Judge Bennet and his frau."

"How do they feel about your enlistment in the Marines, Joe?"

"How do any parents feel? They wouldn't have me not go, but I figure they have let-down moments. I'm their one and only."

"When do you leave?"

"I'm off to New York with Griff at noon. Then on to Washington. I'll have to get his papers in order for a new secretary before I am marching to the tune of 'From the Halls of Montezuma.'"

"I shall miss you. Even in this short time I have come to regard you as a trusty adviser."

"I'll be back on leave. And there is a U.S. mail delivered at Parris Island. Keep me posted. Meanwhile, you'll have Griff and the one and only Gaston Cosgrove to look after you."

"Somehow," Anne told him, "I can't see myself sobbing out my troubles on Mr. Cosgrove's shoulder."

"Is that what you are looking for? A wailing wall? Try Griff."

"I've been told he's a woman-hater."

Joe grinned at her. "Why don't you do a little research and find out? Here we are at the pharmacy. Lucky for you. I was getting so hungry I could bite, and you are the nearest edible."

"The last time I saw this," Anne said, "I was wildly excited. That was the afternoon when I stopped to ask the way to Mountain Lodge."

"That was the day you thought you had been followed, wasn't it? Ever find out who it was—if anyone?"

"I have an idea," she said cautiously. "Good morning, Mr. Marston," she greeted the proprietor who came from behind the screen. "You know Joe Bennet, of course." She sniffed. "I smell coffee. We've had no breakfast. May we order?"

"Sure. Stella!"

In answer to his call a girl with tight black curls and a permanent dimple sidled from behind the screen.

"Good morning, Miss Kendrick. Joe Bennet, *where* did you come from? I haven't seen you for years."

"I'm here with our Congressman for a few days. How about coffee and rolls for two? Stella—you are Stella Moffit, aren't you?"

"That's right. Coffee and rolls for two coming up. Marmalade for you, Miss Kendrick?"

"No, thank you."

The waitress hurried away, each little black curl bobbing in a direction all its own. The proprietor took her place by the table. He looked toward the screen, from behind which came the clink of silver on china, the scent of coffee, the sizzling of boiling water.

"Have you seen Minna Dodge lately, Joe?" he asked, lowering his voice.

"Minna? I'd forgotten she was in the world. Last I heard, she was caught in the New York whirlpool. What brought her to mind?"

"Do you remember Pedro Brocchi, the son of the village fruit man? He was in your class at high school."

"I remember him. Smart as a steel trap."

"So smart that he almost took my shirt supplying him with free ice cream," Marston admitted. "After you left here, he went around with Minna Dodge quite a lot. The reason I asked was that he dropped in here for coffee a couple of hours ago. Looked as if he had been up all night. I had a curious hunch his presence was tied up with the Dodge girl." He broke off as Stella sidled from behind the screen with a laden tray.

"It is grand to see you, Joe." Marston bowed to Anne. "I hope you'll drop in often, Miss Kendrick." He walked toward the rear of the store and disappeared behind a door marked OFFICE.

The waitress set the dishes on the table and stood with the shining tray under her arm, primed for conversation.

"I didn't know who you were when you stopped in the other day, Miss Kendrick. I should have, too, because everyone's been talking about you. But no one had said you were so pretty."

As Anne began to drink her coffee, Stella asked curiously, "Did that good-looking man from the Inn ever catch up with you?"

"What man?" Anne asked idly. She shook her head as Joe, an eager light in his eyes, began to speak.

"The tall blond one driving the swanky dark-green car. He told me he thought he recognized your voice. Sounded like a friend of his. He left right after you did and I thought—"

Joe saw that Anne had no intention of satisfying the girl's curiosity.

"I thought I recognized those black curls, Stella," he said. "I haven't seen you since freshman days. How is the world treating you?"

"Swell. Say, it's funny you should pop in today. I just saw another old classmate of ours. Pedro Brocchi came for coffee this morning. I hadn't seen him since the days when he carried Minna Dodge's schoolbooks. I was talking to him just like I'm talking to you and he snapped, 'I've an important deal on hand. Scram.' "

"Don't let it impress you, Stella. People don't pick out a drugstore to talk important business in."

"Oh, he didn't meet anyone here. He was watching the door the whole time. Then he gave a kind of gasp, threw some money for his coffee on the table, and ran out."

"See who it was?" Joe asked casually.

"When I got to the door he was just driving off. Seemed to be in an awful hurry."

XI

IT WAS ten-twenty-five by the small clock on the Governor Winthrop desk when Anne opened the door of the room Mayme Williams had called her office and which Anne now called her workroom. Some day she would tackle the bookshelves, clear out the books belonging to the previous owner and install her own, she thought. There was such a lot of readjusting to be done.

I arrived Thursday afternoon and this is only Saturday morning, she reminded herself. I've heard tell that Rome wasn't built in a day, she reminded the girl who smiled encouragement from the gilt-framed mirror.

"Come in," she called in answer to a knock on the door.

"You are prompt, Mrs. Dodge," she said pleasantly to the flat-chested woman who entered from the gallery. "Sit down."

"It is part of my job to be prompt," Harriet Dodge declared primly. She sat on the chair Anne had indicated and smoothed her black-and-white dotted print over her angular knees. Her mouth had the martyr's droop. Her eyes were on the thumbs she was twisting one within the other.

Ugh. Uriah Heep in skirts, Anne thought, and was immediately ashamed of her snap judgment.

"I brought my account book in case you wish to check on my honesty." For an instant the heavy lids lifted and revealed eyes that were so colorless and so antagonistic that Anne's heart skipped a beat.

It was not entirely her expression that sent the blood surging to Anne's face. It was her use of the word "case." It hissed like a rattlesnake. The gap left by a missing lower front tooth was responsible for the exaggerated *s* sound. It was Harriet Dodge who had threatened her on the night of her arrival.

She mustn't guess that I know, Anne thought. She withdrew her fascinated gaze from the woman's mouth and opened a notebook on the desk before which she sat.

"I didn't ask you to come here in order to check on your honesty, Mrs. Dodge," she said crisply. "That is the responsibility of Mr. Cosgrove and the trustees of Mrs. Williams's estate. What I want to know is how many persons are employed in the house and what they are paid. That information comes under the head of your department, doesn't it?"

"The estate pays all the bills. It isn't your business to know anything about it." The protest buzzed with hisses.

57

"I consider it my business. I intend to know what it costs to run this house. Do you plan the menus and order the provisions?"

"Why? Aren't the meals satisfactory? Mrs. Williams never complained."

Anne realized that the interview was being made as difficult as possible. With the midnight threat prickling like a splinter in her memory she had expected opposition from some direction. But why did Mrs. Dodge want to get her out of the house? What could she gain by it?

She kept her temper and answered quietly, "The menus are satisfactory and the cooking is excellent. But time is flying and I have a date for tennis at eleven. I want the names and wages of the employees you hire in the house."

Harriet Dodge opened her book. With maddening slowness she spelled out the names and gave the amount paid each employee in the house. Anne kept an iron grip on her rising impatience.

"That is an excellent report, Mrs. Dodge. I realize that you cannot estimate what the cost of food will be, with steadily rising prices and the fact that I haven't been here long enough for you to know what I like. But in the future I want all monthly house bills submitted to me."

"The trustees won't like it."

Anne got up. "That will be all for now, Mrs. Dodge. On Monday morning at eleven I would like to have you show me over the house from top to bottom."

"Very well, Miss Kendrick." Harriet Dodge turned with the knob of the door of the gallery in her hand. "I suppose you'll take that over too. Sounds as if you intended to stay here." Her heavy lids lifted to show a glint of yellow snake-like eyes. Anne repressed a shiver.

"Monday at eleven, Mrs. Dodge." Anne's voice was gay. "We'll begin with the rooms on the first floor. Good morning."

The door remained open for a moment as if the woman were considering a reply, then it closed softly, very softly.

Anne drew a sigh of relief. That was that, and *mirabile dictu,* she had kept her temper.

As she changed to white tennis clothes she wondered if she had been unnecessarily conscientious when she had asked for the names and wages of her employees. *No.* Her experience in the care and upkeep of a house had been limited, but ordinary common sense indicated that a homemaker should know whom she was employing and what she was spending. Hadn't Cosgrove warned her that her income would be decreased by new taxes? Because there was money behind her, why waste it? There was plenty of good to be done with it in this grim new world.

She tied a filmy apple-green kerchief over her hair, threw a matching cardigan across her shoulders. Perfect day, she thought, as she approached the tennis courts. It was still cool, still sparkling in the light and shadow cast by majestically sailing cloud ships. Clarissa Trent, with a lilac kerchief on her white hair, was smashing experimental balls over the net and into it.

"Sorry to be late," Anne said as she joined her. "I had a conference with Mrs. Dodge and she was as slow in her answers as she could be and still move her lips. But I got what I wanted without a burst of temperament on my part. I wonder why that woman hates me."

As Clarissa smiled without answering, she went on, "Stop batting those balls. I bet you know what it's all about. It's only fair to tell me what I'm up against."

"I agree with you. Griff will wring my neck, figuratively speaking, for telling you. He says she'll realize which side her bread is buttered on and settle down to give you A-1 service. She's just carrying on to you her feud with Mrs. Williams."

"What caused it?"

"Jimmy Williams," Clarissa said unexpectedly. "He ran after Minna Dodge for a while. His stepmother was furious. I suspect she had a mental picture of Dodge in the saddle at Mountain Lodge. She was pretty sure the Dodges had Minna around just for that purpose. I don't know what actually happened, but Minna went to New York and Jimmy continued to spend his leaves at Mountain Lodge, apparently in perfect harmony with Mrs. Williams. Harriet Dodge may think her daughter should be in your place. Well, that's that. Don't let it bother you. We two have been standing beside the net talking like two neighbors across a fence. Let's play. Rough or smooth?" She flung down her racket.

"Smooth," Anne called, and won. "I'll take this court." She batted a ball up and down. "The surface is perfect, isn't it?"

"It is. You'll find that everything on the place is in perfect condition. Mrs. Williams left instructions that the estate was to be kept up. She——" Clarissa broke off, her lips white. "You have guests, Anne," she said stiffly. "Where in heaven's name did Ned Crane manage to pick up Sharon?"

Anne turned in surprise to see the tall man and the young girl, both in white tennis clothes, approaching the court, their hands locked together, swinging as they walked.

Clarissa added in a low tone, "Sharon adored Ned at the time he—we were engaged. She was only a little girl then. Don't let him—Anne, Griff and I are responsible for Sharon—break that up every chance you get. Please. Please. *Please.*"

"Pull yourself together, Rissa. Don't let Ned Crane see that

59

you are frightened. It might give him ideas." She went forward to meet the man and the young girl.

"Lovely of you to come to welcome me, Sharon," she said cordially, as though she had not observed the girl's discourtesy at the country club.

Sharon blushed with embarrassment. "Ned came to Forest Edge," she said. "When I told him Aunt Rissa was going to play tennis with you, he suggested that we come and take you on." The explanation had been slightly breathless. "Believe me, I'm quite good, Miss Kendrick." Her large eyes shone like clear brown diamonds as they met Anne's.

"That sounds like fun to me. Shall we take on the challengers, Rissa?"

"We'll show them," Clarissa called merrily. "Choose your court."

"Smooth," Sharon called as her aunt flung down her racket.

"Smooth wins," Rissa declared. "Which court?" As Sharon and Ned Crane established themselves on the other side of the net, she added under her breath, "Go to it, Anne. Knock his block off."

One hilarious ripple of laughter escaped Anne's lips because the remark was so out of character with the dignified Miss Trent of Forest Edge.

She glanced at Crane and regretted that outbreak of laughter. This was the second time she had laughed at the wrong moment. She knew he had heard it and realized it was about himself. Dark color mounted to his hair. She knew he was remembering the last time he had heard her laugh, just before he sailed ignominiously over the wall.

He served a ball with such savage force and accuracy that she could not touch it.

"Fifteen love," he called and served another like it.

At the finish of a set in favor of the challengers, Anne dropped to a bench.

"Do you concede defeat, Rissa? We do. Sharon, you belong among the crowned heads of the tennis world. You were a demon player."

Crane lighted a cigarette. "She was. Pity the annual tournament is over. She and I might have walked off with the honors."

"Excuse me, Anne, but I must go," Clarissa said. "I want to see Griff before he leaves. Sharon—"

"I came with Ned," Sharon began hastily. There was stubbornness in her face.

"As you like," her aunt said helplessly.

"Unless you go right away you won't see Joe before he goes into the Marines," Anne said.

"Joe! In the Marines?" Sharon was on the verge of tears. "Hurry, Aunt Rissa, or we may miss him."

"Come again," Anne called, acknowledging Sharon's farewell wave.

Rissa's lips shaped the words, "Thank you."

Anne turned slowly to find Ned Crane watching her. "It begins to look," he said, "as though you and I were pairing off the wrong way."

"What do you mean?"

"I thought it was you and me," he said. "Now it looks as though it is you and Trent—and me with Sharon—"

"But she is years younger than you are."

"She doesn't seem to mind that."

Anne thought furiously. "Break it up, *please*," Rissa had begged her. She lifted her head and smiled at him. "I'm off for the village," she said.

"Let me take you," he begged as she had expected.

"Thanks. That would be fun."

As they walked in silence toward his car, three scarlet leaves drifted lazily across the path. A bird in a tree chirped monotonously. A gray squirrel chattered a defiant reply. Anne was deep in thought. Ned Crane had tried to marry Rissa Trent and something had gone wrong. Then he had tried to marry her. Now, almost as though he were challenging her, he was deliberately attracting young Sharon.

Sharon, Anne remembered, owned a third of the Trent mill fortune. As for her, Ned Crane had never met her until word had appeared in the papers of the great fortune Mrs. Williams had left her. Had it been the Williams money that attracted him? He seemed to be very sure that he could marry Sharon if he wanted to do so.

She stole a glance at the handsome man with the all-conquering air striding along beside her. She was remembering the crash when this same lord of creation landed in the shrubs.

When they reached the village he helped her out of the car. Behind it another one drew up. Griff Trent and Joe Bennet looked in surprise from her to Ned Crane.

The latter smiled down at her. "Don't be too long, darling," he said, his voice loud in the quiet village street.

XII

THE NIGHT CLUB was a trifle on the flashy side, Griff Trent decided, as, to the accompaniment of the soft strum of guitars, he followed the maître d'hôtel to a table at one end of the space cleared for dancing. There were many middle-

61

aged couples apparently out on their weekly binge sprinkled among the younger patrons. His face, which had been rather grim, lighted up in a laugh as he looked at Bennet sitting across from him.

"You look so darned surprised," he said.

"When you said you had an important date in New York and wanted me to accompany you, I didn't expect to end up at a night club," Joe admitted.

"What are you complaining about? I looked it up. It's listed as Small and Cheerful."

"Cheerful, all right. It blazes with color. The backdrop, I take it, is the façade of a palace in Spain and we are seated in the palm garden, if palaces in Spain sport palm gardens. I wouldn't know. I like the way the strings are making with that Spanish fandango. Two."

He dropped a bill on the flower tray presented by a dark-eyed Carmen, selected two white carnations and pushed one across the table.

"Here you are, Griff. A flower in the lapel of your dinner jacket is indicated."

"Thanks." Trent fastened the boutonniere in place.

"Whom are we to meet here?" Bennet said in growing curiosity. "It has something to do with that telephone call that startled you so at Forest Edge."

"It has," Trent said grimly. "Something very queer is going on, Joe."

"But who—"

"I don't know who it is we're to meet here."

Seeing Joe's growing bewilderment, Trent smiled in spite of his increasing gravity. "She asked me to meet her here—"

"She?"

"Her name is Señorita Lola. Her legal name—" Trent paused for a moment—"is Mrs. Williams."

Mrs.—"

"Keep your voice down. The woman claimed that she is Jimmy Williams's widow. Now you know as much as I do."

"But what does she want with you?"

"I don't know. That's why I want you as a witness to this interview. Whoever she is, I have a hunch there is trouble in the offing."

"Trouble for you?"

"Trouble," Griff said, "for Anne Kendrick—No, don't ask me anything else, Joe. I don't know the answers. We've just got to wait and see what the mysterious Señorita Lola has up her sleeve."

The service and food were excellent. Puzzled as both men were by developments, they enjoyed the stage show. They laughed with a rapid-fire humorist, watched a man, and a woman in a floating green net frock, dance the rumba to the music of a band. Trent began to be impatient. The rumba brass blared itself out. The strings took over. A small balcony in the imitation palace front was spotlighted. Señorita Lola was announced and made her appearance.

A woman in a glittering silver sequin frock with a black mantilla over blond hair began to sing. That the singer was a favorite was evidenced by the thunder of applause that greeted her appearance. To Griff's trained ear she altered pitch and rhythm at will, which resulted in a contrived effect, but she was lovely to look at, her voice was sweet, and she had personality plus.

Joe Bennet's eyes threatened to pop from his head as he looked at Trent. "Griff," he whispered excitedly, "I've seen that girl somewhere before. I know I have."

Griff nodded his head. "Yes," he said in an odd tone, "you have seen her before. Of course, she's changed a lot."

"Who is she?"

"Minna Dodge!"

"Well, I'll be—she has certainly changed from the little country girl I knew. She's built that wisp of a voice into a property."

The blond woman had finished her songs, and now she was weaving her way among the tables, smiling at the applause that followed her. She came straight to Griffith Trent.

He got to his feet and drew out a chair for her. "Well, this is a surprise, Minna."

She smiled at him with professional poise and charm but her hands were trembling.

"Good evening, Mr. Trent. Thank you for coming." She looked at Joe Bennet. "Hello, Joe. It's a long time since I've seen you. But, Mr. Trent, I asked you to come for a private conversation."

Joe started to get up but Griff said, "Sit down. Joe is my secretary. I have no confidences from him." As Minna Dodge —or, apparently, Mrs. Jimmy Williams—hesitated, Griff added firmly, "Joe sits in on this conference or I step out. Do you agree to that?"

She flung out her hands helplessly. "What choice do I have?" she said bitterly.

Griff studied her in open curiosity. A few years had done a great deal for the flaxen-haired little high-school girl. She had become an extremely attractive young woman. The pale hair was a golden brown. The giggling, awkward school girl had become a poised and charming woman. Yes, she had come a long way.

But watching her, Griff was reminded of Anne Kendrick, with her simple, uncalculated manners, her warm unstudied

63

graciousness, her gaiety of spirit, the eyes that met his squarely and honestly. Anne was genuine and real. Behind this sophisticated girl's manner everything was calculated, planned to the last gesture. Behind the nervousness she could not conceal there was a cold intelligence at work.

"Over the telephone," he said, "you told me that you were Jimmy Williams's widow."

She nodded. She lifted a lacy handkerchief to her dry eyes. "Poor Jimmy," she said. "Poor Jimmy."

"Why have you waited so long to explain that you are—were—his wife?"

"How could I," she demanded, "while Mrs. Williams was alive? She never liked me. She would have cut him out of her will if she had known. And that—" she broke off and her crisp tone changed, became pathetic— "and that wouldn't have been fair to Jimmy. I loved him too much to hurt him."

"But," Griff reminded her, "even before Jimmy's death was established, Mrs. Williams had made it clear that she would leave him no money at all. You must have known that. She made no secret of the fact."

"But she might have changed her mind," Minna said quickly. Again her tone altered. "And Jimmy didn't want to hurt her. Because she disapproved of me so terribly. I guess I wasn't good enough for her."

"Do your parents know about this?"

"No," she said quickly. Too quickly. "I never told them. Up to now, I've never told a soul."

"Then why do it now? And why," Griff asked, "come to me with this—story?"

"Because," she said, "I haven't any money and I need it badly. Jimmy would have hated that. When he went into the air force—before we were married—he took out ten thousand dollars' insurance. That was all he had to leave. It went to Mrs. Williams. It seems to me that I have a right to that, at least. He would have wanted me to have it. Heaven knows, *she* didn't need it." There was venom in that *she.* "It's only fair, Mr. Trent—just Jimmy's insurance money—"

Griff didn't hear the rest of that sentence. Ten thousand dollars, she had said. And ten thousand dollars, in new hundred-dollar bills, had been withdrawn from the bank by Mrs. Williams the morning of the day she died. And had never been seen since then. Coincidence? Well, maybe. But Griff had little faith in coincidence.

He leaned forward, his fine, strong face serious, his eyes forcing her to look at him.

"Minna," he said, "before her death you told Mrs. Williams about your marriage."

"How did you know?" Her surprise was a confession.

64

Many of the missing pieces of the puzzle slipped into place.

"You called on her a few days before she died, didn't you?"

He sounded so confident that she didn't attempt to lie. "Yes, I did."

"Then your parents did know."

She shook her head. "They had a day off together. I chose that day to go to Mountain Lodge."

"What did you say to Mrs. Williams?"

"I told her Jimmy and I had been secretly married. Then after he was—lost—" again she made a play with her handkerchief— "I had to get a night-club job to support myself. Then I found it hard to get along. So I asked for Jimmy's insurance."

"What did she say?"

Minna was surprised. "I expected she would be furious," she said frankly. "Instead, she seemed to be terribly hurt. She kept saying, 'I didn't think Jimmy would do that to me. I thought he was the one person left who really loved me—but you don't deceive people whom you really love.' Then she began to get that Great Lady air of hers. She said, 'Do your parents know about this?' And I was afraid for them, afraid they would lose their jobs. So I lied—I—"

"Then they do know," Griff said quietly.

"You always know everything, don't you?" There was bitterness in her tone.

"Do you have any children?" Griff asked.

"No."

"Did Mrs. Williams say she would give you the insurance money?"

"She asked me for proof," Minna said. "She said, 'Of course, you know you have no legal claim on me or my estate.' I said I wasn't trying to make a claim. But since Jimmy's insurance had been paid to her, I thought—knowing he would want me to have it—"

"Do you have any proof of your marriage?"

Minna studied Griff's face but it revealed nothing.

"I had my marriage certificate, and like a fool I left it with her so that she could make her own investigation and prove it was true. She said she would look into it, and if we had really been married, she would send me ten thousand dollars. The last thing she said was, 'You will hear from me. But keep this strictly between ourselves.' I promised, of course, and she said, 'See if you can keep this promise.' The next afternoon she was dead."

"Why did you send for me?" Griff said.

"There was no one else I could trust absolutely. Jimmy always regarded you as his best friend. I thought—she did

65

promise me the money, you know—and I need it badly—"

"And the wedding certificate?"

"It's gone. As I told you, I left it with Mrs. Williams. It was not returned to me." She looked down at a diamond watch bracelet on her wrist. "I have another number in a few moments. I must go now. You will help me, won't you?"

Joe, who had been listening intently, followed a hunch and spoke up for the first time. "But why Griff?" he asked. "Why don't you page your old friend, Pedro Brocchi? He'd do anything to help you."

The lacy handkerchief ripped as her fingers pulled convulsively at it. For a moment the two men thought she was going to faint. Then, summoning up a smile, she nodded to them and walked swiftly away.

They stood watching her go. "Sit down, Joe," Griff said, realizing that they were attracting attention. "Who is Pedro Brocchi that the very mention of his name should do that to her?"

Bennet told him about his visit to the pharmacy with Anne and what both Tim Marston and Stella had said about Pedro Brocchi's unexpected appearance in his old home town.

"Do you think it was Pedro who gave her that diamond wrist watch?" Griff asked.

Joe shook his head. "Unless times have changed greatly for Pedro, he doesn't make that kind of money."

"But someone is spending a great deal of money on Minna," Griff said thoughtfully.

"Do you believe her story?"

"Figure it out for yourself," Griff said. "She claims to have left proof of her marriage with Aunt Mayme. That proof—along with a will, a gray parrot, and ten thousand dollars—has disappeared. Doesn't it strike you that too many things are missing from Mountain Lodge?"

"Oh, that reminds me, about the parrot—" Joe began but Griff had gone on, "Minna is not hard up, Joe. She is making a big salary in a place like this. And someone is buying her diamonds. She was lying when she said she needed that ten thousand dollars."

"Then, why," Joe asked, bewildered, "did she come to you with that story?"

"That," Griff told him firmly, "is what we have got to find out."

XIII

ANNE KENDRICK sat at the desk in her workroom, unseeing eyes on the great sweep of valley and mountain, brilliant with color. The sky was a deep arch of blue but already there was a touch of winter in the air. The ground was carpeted deep in red and orange, in russet and brown and gold. Here and there the branches of the trees were stark.

Inside, a gay little fire crackled under the mantel while Anne, in cherry-red pullover, cardigan and matching plaid skirt, sat at her desk nibbling her pen.

Below her window she could see asters, calendulas, and glads, all the autumn flowers in the garden, blooming their heads off as though determined to put on their best show before the impending frost nipped them.

I have so much to be thankful for, she kept telling herself. All this beauty around me, stretching as far as my eyes can see, and this wonderful house.

It's no use, she decided, putting down her pen, I can't go on pretending. The house is lovely but I am afraid of it.

She tried to shake off her dark thoughts and make herself remember what she had accomplished during the past week. I might be excused for being frightened at night, particularly after that scary warning, but not in the daytime, not now with the light sparkling over everything. This is my home and I might as well get used to living in it. After all, there is nothing to be afraid of but my own imagination. Since I shut off the connection between the rooms I haven't heard that awful voice. Everything is all right.

She had managed to cheer herself a little and she sat back, recalling her trip of investigation through the house, with Mrs. Dodge grudgingly opening every door as though Anne had no right to enter the rooms. At least, Anne thought, the Dodges didn't dare say anything when I had the changes made, when I had those three doors opened on the first floor and the linen shrouds taken off the furniture and hangings. The whole entertaining suite looked ghostly that first day, the windows dark, the furniture like sheeted figures. Now it is what it should be, pale-gold brocade at the long windows in the hall and dining room, opening on a flagged terrace. The walls a Williamsburg green. Crystal chandeliers, circa 1880, all very elegant, all very before World War II.

There are really too many things. I'll ask the trustees about holding an old-fashioned auction with coffee, cheese and crackers, the proceeds to go to the veterans' hospital.

Only one strange thing had happened during that trip of investigation. When Anne and Mrs. Dodge had completed their inspection of the house from top to bottom Mrs. Dodge had said, "Well, I guess you've seen all there is."

Anne tried to conceal the shiver of revulsion she experienced whenever the housekeeper spoke, the hissing of *s*'s reminding her of that first night's terror.

"Oh, there's one thing more, Mrs. Dodge. The closet in *my* suite—" she couldn't help accenting that word *my* as a sign of independence— "is filled with Mrs. Williams's clothes. I'll need the space for my own wardrobe. We'll have to clean it out as soon as possible."

Mrs. Dodge's eyes glittered. "You can't get in without a key and the trustees locked up all Mrs. Williams's personal possessions as soon as she died."

"I'll get the key," Anne said. "Mr. Dunn is sending it to me."

All week Mrs. Dodge must have been watching because she had been on hand when the key arrived. As Anne turned it in the lock of the long closet, which ran almost the length of her bedroom, she could hear the housekeeper's rasping breathing. The woman was so close that she was touching her.

Then the door opened and a light switched on. For a moment Anne looked in dismay at the dozens of satin-padded hangers, at the clothes neatly arranged—suits, sports clothes, evening dresses, afternoon dresses—at the shelves of hat boxes and shoe boxes.

"Oh, dear," she exclaimed in dismay. "I can never go through all that."

"Mrs. Williams promised me," the housekeeper said, her voice suddenly hoarse, "that I could have her clothes when she died."

Anne hesitated. Perhaps it was true. The Dodges had been with Mrs. Williams for many years. And what could be done with the clothes? Give them to the poor? After all, she had practically promised Gaston Cosgrove that she would turn them over to Mrs. Dodge and he had said it was what Mrs. Williams would have wished.

She was perplexed and tired. All week long she had handled problems in regard to the house and discussed investments with the trustees in the absence of Gaston Cosgrove, who had gone to New York to see the people who wanted to buy houses on her property. She did not want to make any more decisions for a while.

"All right," she agreed. "But try to get the closet cleaned out today."

68

"I will." Mrs. Dodge stretched out her long bony arms and began to load them with dresses, working in almost feverish haste. Spots of color burned in her cheeks. There was something odd about her, something almost triumphant.

"Wait," Anne said suddenly. "I'll go through them first." As Mrs. Dodge stood quite still Anne was conscious of a pang of fear as though danger threatened her. But that was silly, she thought. No one was there—no one but Mrs. Dodge.

Slowly the housekeeper put the dresses back on their hangers. She stood waiting.

"That's all, Mrs. Dodge," Anne said, trying to speak lightly. "I'll send for you when I've looked over the clothes."

For a moment the housekeeper seemed about to speak. Then her lips closed in a tight, thin line and she went out, shutting the door noiselessly behind her.

An instinct Anne hardly understood made her walk silently to the door and turn the key in the lock.

For a moment she looked helplessly at the huge, cluttered closet and then she got to work. The troble was that she had no idea what she was looking for. She climbed on a slipper chair and started with the hatboxes. The shoe boxes came next. Finally, she began to examine the dresses one by one, looking in the pockets.

Careful as she was, she almost missed it. She was shaking out a gray silk dress before adding it to the toppling pile on her bed. The light caught a faint bulge on one side of the skirt and her groping fingers found a concealed pocket she had missed. She withdrew a slip of paper and carried it to the light.

Scrawled on it was a memorandum: *Have G.C. hire a detective to check.*

At length the closet was empty and there was nothing else. But why had the Dodges been so desperately eager to get hold of the memorandum? Dodge had tried to prevent her from using the rooms, his wife had been furious when she had insisted on investigating the contents of the closet.

Anne's troubled thoughts broke off. The handle of the door was turning silently. She watched it in fascination, one shaking hand at her throat. Then it moved back into place again. She held her breath but she heard nothing. There had been no sound of steps in the hall.

She forced herself to call, "Who is it?"

No one answered.

At length she went to the door, drew a long breath, turned the key and flung the door open. The hall was empty. With a shiver of fear Anne left the bedroom and went into her workroom, trying to assemble her thoughts.

Now what? Big as the house was, it seemed to be closing in on her. Anne left her desk, caught up her beige topcoat and ran down the stairs. Out of doors she paused for a moment, drawing into her lungs the crisp autumn air, feeling the sun warm on her head. To whom could she go? Her lawyer was in New York. Anyhow, as she had told Joe Bennet, she could not cry on Cosgrove's shoulder.

What had he replied? "You'd better try Griff."

But Griffith Trent was in Washington. He would not be back for at least another week. Rissa—Anne hesitated. She had not seen Griff's sister since the day of the tennis party.

Abruptly, Anna started along the path through the woods that led to Forest Edge, her hands thrust deep in the pockets of her coat. *Have G.C. hire a detective to check.* Why should that message be so important to the Dodges? Perhaps they hadn't been looking for that. Perhaps they thought the missing ten thousand dollars was in that locked closet.

G.C. Gaston Cosgrove, of course. But why was he to hire a detective? To check on her? Mrs. Williams had already done that. Griffith Trent had handled her detective work. And she hadn't wanted her lawyer to know it.

Anne walked faster. It would help to talk to someone.

But when the maid ushered her into the room where Clarissa Trent was pouring tea before an open fire, she was disappointed to see that her hostess was not alone. She was serving tea to the luscious brunette who had sat at the Trent table at the country club, the one who had called Griff "darling."

As the maid announced her, both women looked up with the same expression of eagerness and both faces fell. Anne's cheeks flamed with embarrassment.

Then Rissa, in a lavender wool dress with a short bolero, came running to meet her, holding out both hands.

"Welcome, Anne! Welcome to Forest Edge." Her warmth made Anne think she had imagined the shadow on her face, and then Rissa explained in a low tone, "I thought at first Sharon had come back. She's been gone all afternoon and she didn't tell—"

She broke off. "Anne, I want you and Mrs. Mason to know each other. Zoe, this is Miss Kendrick, the new owner of Mountain Lodge."

There was no reflection of Clarissa's glowing friendship on Zoe Mason's face. A deep rose suit dress clung to the beautiful, languorous figure. The hand she extended so lazily was glittering with rings. Her sultry eyes studied Anne.

"I have heard a great deal about you, Miss Kendrick," she said in an attractively husky voice. "Now and then I used to

70

see your television program. How does it feel to inherit a fortune?"

Anne smiled without attempting a reply.

Clarissa broke in eagerly. "Choosing Anne to take her place was one of the wisest things Aunt Mayme ever did."

"I understand a husband goes with the estate," Zoe said, watching Anne from under lowered lids.

"Where on earth did you hear that?"

"A little bird," Zoe said. "With that much money I should think you could find a husband of your own."

"Zoe!" Clarissa protested angrily.

Zoe laughed. "I was only joking, Rissa. Miss Kendrick can marry any man she likes so long as there's no poaching. When will Griff be back?"

Anne felt her cheeks burning. Zoe Mason had established her claim clearly enough.

Clarissa was angry but she was a trained hostess. She shifted the conversation.

"Anne, when will you be ready to start work as an ambulance driver?"

"Tomorrow," Anne told her.

She was bitterly disappointed. But I can't talk about the Dodges and that strange memorandum in Mrs. Williams's pocket before Mrs. Mason, she thought.

Clarissa eagerly made plans and Anne found herself relaxing. The fears that were so real at Mountain Lodge dissolved like smoke in this friendly atmosphere. Even Zoe, watching but taking no part in the conversation, could not detract from her relief.

The maid appeared at the door, followed by Parson Savage. After greeting his hostess, he bowed to Zoe Mason and took Anne's hand.

"I don't need any introduction to this young lady," he said, smiling down at her. "I am one of her trustees. Anyhow, I have been hearing a lot about you, Miss Kendrick. How have you managed, in so few days, to make so many people fall in love with you? The village children have been telling me that you stop to play with them and tell them stories. You are making a real place for yourself here."

"Thank you," she said huskily.

"And tomorrow," Clarissa told him, "she is going to start driving the wounded from the airfield to the veterans' hospital."

"I hope," Zoe said, irritated by praise directed to someone else, "you aren't going to bring in people who will change the character of this part of the country."

"What on earth do you mean?" Anne asked in surprise.

Zoe shrugged slim shoulders. "I've noticed some strange-looking people around this week. I heard they were looking at the property you have for sale."

"Mr. Cosgrove handles that," Anne said. "I am sure he can be trusted not to sell to anyone who would cause trouble here."

Zoe laughed. "Mr. Cosgrove," she said, "would sell to anyone he was sure would pay his commission. You don't seem to know our slippery and ambitious Gaston. I always wondered how he fooled a smart woman like Mrs. Williams. He must have hypnotized her."

There was a sound of laughing voices and Sharon came bursting in from the terrace, like a flicker of sunshine, in a pale-yellow sweater and skirt, a yellow ribbon tied around her dark curls, followed by Ned Crane in brown slacks and a deep-blue sweater.

The smile faded from Clarissa's face. For a moment Crane's eyes met Anne's in a bold challenge and then he bowed easily. Clarissa answered coldly. Zoe, who had been lolling in her chair, sat up at the sight of a handsome stranger and acknowledged the introduction with a smile and a glitter of rings as she held out her hand.

"Sharon—" Clarissa's voice was crisp—"you didn't tell me where you were going."

"I'm sorry, Aunt Rissa. I met Ned when I was walking in the woods and we got to talking and—I—just forgot the time."

"The fault is all mine." Crane was obviously pleased with himself. "Sharon is such fun to talk to—" His eyes rested on the girl's face and Anne saw the soft color rise on her cheeks. For a moment her eyes met Clarissa's. Both of them had felt this man's fascination. How could a seventeen-year-old girl escape it?

Clarissa is watching her step, Anne thought. She doesn't dare refuse to receive Ned. It would only make Sharon defend him. And Ned won't give up. He warned me that day at the pharmacy when he called, "Don't be too long, darling," so that Griff and Joe would hear him. He laughed when I protested at that. Laughed when I demanded, "Why did you follow me up here?"

He hadn't denied it. "Because I don't intend to lose you, Anne." He had become deadly serious. "Why did you refuse to see me again?"

It was difficult to say, "I can't trust you. I think you are faithless. You could not be true to a woman for all your life."

"Because it's no use," she had said.

His hand had held hers in a crushing grip. "For the last time, Anne, will you marry me?"

She had pulled her hand away. "For the last time, no."

That day he had driven her back to Mountain Lodge in silence. When he helped her out of the car he said, "I always get what I want. I never give up. If not one way, then another."

It seemed almost as though he were talking to himself rather than to her. Anne had gone into the house without making any reply. For a week she had seen and heard nothing of him. But now she knew what he had been doing. Transferring his attentions to Sharon Ames—or to Sharon Ames's fortune?

Later, on the path through the woods, on her way home from Forest Edge, Anne wished she had not been so quick to say she didn't mind walking. The sky was glorious in the west but there was only dusk on the path.

She walked quickly, her coat turned up around her neck, hands thrust deep into her pockets. A sudden rustling in the undergrowth made her jump and her heart raced. Just some animal, probably a rabbit, scurrying away. More frightened of me than I am of it, she told herself.

What's the matter with you, Anne Kendrick? she scolded. You jump at every sound. You imagine things. Aren't you ashamed?

She flung back her head and began to sing, the notes soaring clear and lovely in the evening air, a melancholy old French song, "Plaisir d'Amour."

The last notes died away.

Then Anne noticed it, the smell of cigarette smoke in the air. And there was no one in the woods but herself. I won't run, she thought. There's nothing to be afraid of. This is ridi—

She bent over as though to adjust her shoe and looked over her shoulder. There was a firefly only a few yards from her. A firefly? As she watched, it moved up in an arc, a watch dial with illuminated figures, long, modernistic numerals.

She went on, quickening her steps. Behind her there was the sound of a stone rolling as a shoe struck it. It was dark now. She could scarcely make out the path but ahead she could see the lights of Mountain Lodge. The house she had feared only an hour before seemed like a refuge.

She broke into a run, blundering against undergrowth, nearly falling as the path turned. The feet behind her were pounding along the path now.

Her breath labored in her chest. Her legs seemed too tired to move. She made a final, desperate effort and staggered out of the darkness onto her own lawn, stumbled up the steps and set her finger on the bell.

The racing feet behind her came to a halt. For a moment she saw a dim figure on the path.

There was a blaze of light as Dodge opened the door. Before she went inside Anne looked back. There was no one on the path.

XIV

IN HIS office in the nation's capital, Griffith Trent ushered out the last visitor and returned to his desk. He twisted his chair around and sat staring out the window.

Joe Bennet, his red hair tousled, looked up from the corner desk, where he was busily putting his papers in order before joining the Marines. His face was anxious as he watched his chief.

"I wish you didn't have to give so much of your time to your constituents," he said. "The result is that you work far into the night. You are too tired and worried."

Griff turned around. "I'm not tired," he said, "and I don't grudge the time I give this job. It is worth every minute of it. But you're right, fella, I'm worried."

Joe's eyes were wide with alarm. "Do you think Cosgrove will really win your seat?"

"That is in the hands of the voters. If my record isn't good enough—"

"Yours!" Joe exploded. "I'd like to know how many other representatives have a record like yours. Why—"

"I have your good opinion anyhow," Griff laughed and for a moment the anxious expression left his face. Then it was back again.

"I had a letter from Rissa today. It didn't sound like her at all. She's always so controlled. But this time—I'll be glad to get back to Forest Edge, Joe! It seems to me as though this week will never end. And yet I keep telling myself nothing can happen in the next few days."

"Happen to Rissa?"

"To Anne Kendrick. I think she's in danger, Joe."

"Anne! What danger?"

"If I knew where the danger lay I'd know what to do about it." There was anguish in his tone.

"So it's like that with you?" Joe said slowly.

Griff nodded. "That's the way it is," he said gruffly, "for all my life."

"Did Rissa say something to make you think Anne is in danger?"

"She said Anne came for tea the other day. There were shadows under her eyes and she seemed to be under a strain.

74

Rissa wanted to ask her about it but Zoe was there—anyhow, Anne walked home through the woods and someone followed her. She called Rissa from home and said a man had chased her. Rissa writes that she was breathless but trying gallantly not to sound afraid—"

"Take it easy," Joe said. "She wasn't hurt."

"No, but she might have been."

"Any idea who followed her?"

"That's a queer thing. She sent Dodge out to look around. He was gone over twenty minutes. When he came back he said there was no one near the house. But he had a big bruise on his face which he said he'd got by running into a tree in the dark. Anne told Rissa he was furiously angry and trying to cover it up."

"That's darned queer," Joe admitted. "Dodge! Griff, I heard Dodge trying to take a high hand with Anne before I left. About the last thing she said to me was that she had an interview scheduled with Mrs. Dodge and dreaded it. Do you think they are trying to drive her away on Minna's account?"

"Could be. I don't know what to think," Griff admitted. "They should realize that even if Minna did marry Jimmy Williams she isn't Mrs. Williams's heir."

"Even if? Do I detect suspicion in your tone?"

"You do," Griff declared. "Minna lied to us about needing money, and yet Jimmy's insurance was supposed to be the reason she admitted being his widow. She lied about her parents knowing about her marriage. Why couldn't she have lied about the marriage certificate she claims to have left with Mrs. Williams and that is now supposed to be missing?"

They were silent for a moment. Griff's fingers beat a nervous tattoo on the desk.

"There are too many things missing from that house," he said at last. "Ten thousand dollars in cash, a mysterious will, a marriage certificate, a parrot. You know, Joe, it might be interesting to find out what that parrot overheard in Mrs. Williams's room the day she died."

"That reminds me," Joe said excitedly, "I forgot to tell you about finding Old Soc."

"*Finding—*"

Joe described his discovery of the parrot at the Wingate farm, his talk with Anne at the club, the escape of the eavesdropper after his fall out of the tree, and learning the next morning that the parrot had been stolen. And Joe's crimson muffler had been left at the scene of the theft.

"It was all my fault, Griff," he said. "That guy overheard me shoot off my mouth, telling Anne where Old Soc was. I sure made it easy for him. If I had only been more careful—"

"Don't take it so hard, fella," Griff said. "Anyone might have done the same thing. But this man in the tree—did you catch sight of him?"

Joe shook his head despondently. "I didn't do anything right. It all happened so fast that it took me completely by surprise."

"I wonder if he's the same man who followed Anne home from Rissa's. There's a campaign to drive that girl away from Mountain Lodge, Joe. The first night she arrived someone warned her to get out." He described the message that had come through the grating, while Joe listened, his mouth open.

"Now I begin to see why you're so worried," he said. "Even if you hadn't gone completely off the deep end about her—"

"I hope my state of mind isn't as obvious to her as it is to you."

"Why? She needs someone to look after her."

"I don't want her to marry me for protection. The kind of marriage I want must have more than that. Anyhow, Anne wouldn't marry me—or anyone—on those conditions. You have only to see that steadfast look in those eyes of hers—" He cleared his throat of huskiness. "What we've got to do now, Joe, is to figure out some way to protect her."

"Right you are, Griff," Joe said briskly. "Count me in. But if this marriage of Minna's is behind the trouble Anne is having—"

"We don't know that there ever was such a marriage. I grew up with Jimmy. Unless he changed a lot in the last year he'd never have done an underhand thing like that."

"Then you don't believe in the missing marriage certificate?"

"I'll need proof before I do."

"And how are you going to get it?"

Griff got up and paced the floor, the anxiety fading from his face as he planned a course of action.

"If Minna and Jimmy were married, there will be records somewhere," he thought aloud. "I'm going to hire a detective to make a search. Anyhow, I want to know what Minna is really after. Someone is giving her diamond bracelets. Could that someone be plotting to get hold of the Williams fortune through Minna?"

"Pedro!" Joe exclaimed. He reminded Griff about the boy-and-girl romance between Minna and Pedro Brocchi, and about Stella's account in the drugstore of Pedro's unexpected reappearance in the village.

"So he had a big deal on," Griff said thoughtfully, when Joe had finished. "And Stella did not see whom he drove away with. Now I wonder—"

Joe looked at Griff and started to speak. He hesitated. Cleared his throat.

"What's wrong, Joe?" Griff laughed.

"You aren't the only one to get letters," Joe said, his face crimson with embarrassment. "Sharon wrote to me. She—look, Griff, you know she's just a kid. Warm sympathies. Always on the side of the underdog."

"What are you trying to say?" Griff looked at him in surprise.

"You remember that slick guy Crane who cropped up in the flashy green convertible just before we left; the one we heard call Anne 'darling'?"

"I remember," Griff said grimly.

"Oh, sure, you must know the guy. I remember he danced with Rissa at the country club."

"Confound his impudence! What about him?"

"I don't know what his game is," Joe said, "but he seems to be making a big play for Sharon's sympathies. Told her some fiction about you knocking him over a wall at the country club."

Griff chuckled. "That was no fiction."

"He also told her you tried to ruin his life. The idea planted in Sharon's mind is that you are jealous of him and you even prejudiced Rissa against him. So Sharon is being Crane's champion in a big way."

"I won't have that," Griff said so quietly that at first Joe did not realize how deadly serious he was. "Before I'll let him—"

"Who is this guy anyhow?" Joe asked curiously.

"He is the man Rissa so nearly married four years ago. The day before their engagement was to be announced a man came to see me. He had quite a story. He had been lending money to Ned Crane on which he was making a big splash in Washington society—fancy car, snappy clothes, expensive apartment. The man who came to my office was getting anxious. Crane not only hadn't paid back his loan, he wanted more money to see him through his honeymoon. After that, he assured the moneylender, he'd pay the whole thing. With Rissa's money."

Joe leaped to his feet, his fists clenched. "Why the—I wish I'd known that when—"

"Take it easy. The blow nearly shattered Rissa, of course. She never dreamed it was her money that Crane wanted. She has got over him but she hasn't fully recovered from the hurt. She has never been in Washington since then. When she can come back here I'll know she's cured. . . . The next time Crane appeared in my life," Griff went on, "was when he followed Anne up to—"

"Yes, I found out he was the one who followed her."

"He was. The Williams money this time. And now, having failed with Anne—who has a curious instinct about loyalty; she would be hard to fool—he is going to try for Sharon's third in the Trent money."

"It's queer Rissa's old love should turn up just when Zoe Mason comes back," Joe said with a sidelong glance at Griff.

Griff laughed. "Zoe is ancient history. She jilted me for the man she preferred. We mean nothing to each other now."

"She means nothing to you but—"

Griff shook his head. "Zoe doesn't care about me. She always resented the fact that I spent so much time on the job. She wanted a playboy, not a man with a sense of responsibility for his country and the way it is governed."

"Maybe that's what she wanted then," Joe suggested. He looked at his watch. "I forgot I have an appointment. Take me about fifteen minutes. I'll be back before you leave."

Griff nodded and turned to the papers stacked on his desk. He made an effort of will to put aside his anxiety about Anne and concentrate on the many problems awaiting him on his chosen job.

He had been working for some minutes when he became aware of the scent of perfume. Anne? His thoughts leaped to her at once. But why should it be Anne?

Zoe Mason was standing just inside the door of his office. She wore a gray suit and a smart gray hat like a crown on her dark hair. A mink stole was flung back over her shoulder.

"I've been waiting for you to notice me, darling," she said.

"I'm sorry, Zoe. I was busy."

"I've been waiting a long time for you to notice me," she went on. "A very long time. At Forest Edge you try to put as much distance between us as possible. I thought if I came to Washington and saw you alone—"

She dropped gracefully into the chair across the desk so that they faced each other. "I watched for that red-haired secretary of yours to go out. Otherwise," she laughed bitterly, "you would have made him stay."

As Griff made no reply, she insisted, "Wouldn't you, Griff? So I couldn't talk to you alone."

"We did all our talking a long time ago." He tried to speak lightly. "Remember? You decided I was a dull old drudge—that's a direct quote."

"But, darling—"

"I haven't changed, Zoe."

"Griff! You mean—" she began eagerly.

"I mean I'm still what you would call a drudge. I like my work. I handle my job the best I know how. So far as anything else is concerned—"

"Do you mean me by that cryptic 'anything else'?" Unexpectedly her eyes filled with tears. "I made a mistake, Griff. That's what I've been trying to tell you ever since I came back. I made a bad mistake. It was you I loved all the time."

As she came slowly around the desk toward him, Griff got to his feet. Why on earth didn't Joe come back? What was keeping him?

"Griff!" She stretched out her hands and rested them on his shoulders, looking up into his face. "You're just the same. You said so yourself," she pleaded. "It's not too late for us —" One arm stole up around his neck.

The door opened. "Oh," Joe Bennet said. "Sorry to intrude."

"You aren't intruding," Griff told him in relief. "Mrs. Mason was just going. Will you take her down, Joe, and help her find a cab?"

"Glad to," Joe said.

Zoe's arm dropped to her side. "You *have* changed," she said, her voice suddenly shrill. "Then it's true—what people are saying."

"What are they saying?"

"That you are going to marry Miss Kendrick. That you're the husband Mayme Williams left her. That you'll share in the Williams estate that way."

She started toward the door. "You'd better decide which you want most, Griff: that marriage or your political career."

"What do you mean by that, Zoe?" he asked levelly.

"I mean the voters aren't going to care much for a candidate who lets himself be used like a pawn to marry money."

The door slammed behind her.

"Whew!" Joe exclaimed. "What is it that hath no fury like a woman scorned?"

"What I'd like to know," Griff said slowly, "is who told Zoe that Mayme Williams left Anne a husband."

"Great Scott! It's not really true, is it?"

"Don't be a dope, Joe. Of course it's not true. It was something Anne thought up on the spur of the moment to get rid of Ned Crane. I'm sure Anne never mentioned it to anyone. I know darned well I didn't. So that leaves Ned Crane." He thought for a moment. "Or Dodge, who also heard that very dramatic declaration."

"Ned Crane or Dodge." Joe considered the two names. "Sure there was no one else?"

"Rissa was there but—"

"Of course," Joe agreed. "She wouldn't have mentioned it. If anyone talked, I hope it was Dodge."

"Why?" Griff asked in surprise.

"Because if it is Crane, he might tell that story to Sharon. If he could make her believe you're for sale in the matrimonial market, nothing you could say to her would do much good."

"You're right," Griff said. "You know, Joe, I have a hunch something is going on at Mountain Lodge. Something we ought to stop and stop fast."

"Only a few more days to go," Joe encouraged him, "and then you can fly back. After all, nothing much can happen in a couple of days."

XV

ANNE DID not know what sound had awakened her. Her heart was leaping and pounding, her eyes were wide open, staring into the darkness. She held her breath, listening.

The big house seemed to have come alive in the night. She had a keen awareness of people moving about somewhere near her. But the only sound she could clearly distinguish among the stirring and crackling of old timber common to any aging house, was a sharp clear tap like a woman's high heel on an uncarpeted floor.

Don't get panicky, Anne, she told herself. You've got to *think*. Where—where—I've got it. There are scatter rugs in the bedroom of that nurse-companion's suite I occupied my first night here—ten days ago! Someone stepping on the bare floor. . . . I'm glad I've taken to locking my door at night, though it seems ridiculous in my own house. But I feel safer. Only a little longer and Griffith Trent will be back. I'll ask his advice. The grating! If someone really is in that suite—

She stretched out her hand in the darkness. It touched the grating beside the head of her bed. Groped for the button and pressed it. In a moment a light glowed red. The current was on.

Then, as though someone were standing beside her bed, she heard the voice. A woman's voice, low-pitched and lovely. A voice she had never heard before.

"What are you doing here?"

For a moment Anne thought the question was addressed to her and she nearly answered.

Then a man said, "That's funny, coming from you. What are *you* doing here?"

"Please go away before you cause me any more trouble," the woman pleaded.

The man laughed and the woman said "Sshh!" in a tone of alarm.

"Why don't you call for help?" he taunted her.

The woman's voice was soft, pleading. "I thought you loved me."

"I did," the man said gruffly.

"Then why don't you help me?"

Anne held her breath, listening eagerly. Who on earth were these people and how had they got into the house? Before going to bed she had made the rounds with Dodge herself, to make sure that doors and windows were carefully locked. What was going on at Mountain Lodge?

"Don't worry, Miss Kendrick," Dodge had said, looking grimmer than ever with the bruise on one cheek, "I'll make sure this house is locked up like a jail every night."

Anne had believed him. Since his encounter in the woods—and there had been an encounter; she was sure of that in spite of his denials—he was worried and uneasy.

But two people had managed to break into the house, unknown to each other until they had met by accident in the nurse-companion's vacant rooms.

"Help you? That's a laugh!" the man said roughly.

"I could make trouble for you," the woman warned him. "I don't want to but I could."

"How?"

"You stole that ten thousand dollars."

"My, my, aren't you smart?" he jeered.

"And you took Old Soc, the parrot."

"You're wrong there," he said. "I don't know any more about the parrot than the man in the moon."

"But you do know about the ten thousand dollars," she said quickly.

The man laughed again. "I'm surprised you don't ask me if I also stole the mysterious missing will!"

There was a startled exclamation. Then the woman demanded breathlessly, "What do you know about it?"

"I know *all* about it. Remember that in the future."

"So that's it! Blackmail! I might have known."

"You aren't the only smart cooky around here. Not by a long shot. Well, I'll be seeing you."

"I never want to see you again."

"But you will," the man mocked her. "So long for now."

Anne pulled a black velvet robe around her, concealing the white crepe pajamas, groped for her mules, and crept softly across the room. She looked out of the open window. Farther along the house she saw a hand reach out of a window and clutch the heavy ivy. On the wrist was a watch with an illuminated dial and long, modernistic numbers.

The man on the path!

A dark figure swung out of the window and climbed down

the vine. A rustling told of his progress. He dropped to the ground.

Anne crept back to bed. At least she knew how the man had gotten into the house. But the woman? Through the grating Anne could hear the low sound of her stifled sobbing.

What ought I to do? Anne wondered. Better break the connection before she notices the red light. Her fingers pressed the button and there was silence. Shall I call Dodge? What did they mean about the mysterious will? And blackmail? Is it something Mrs. Williams knew or guessed? Is that why she planned to hire a detective?

"You're not the only smart cooky around here." Smart cooky! That was the new phrase Old Soc had learned.

Joe Bennet thought the man who said "Smart cooky" was the one who had stolen the parrot. But this man denied doing so, although he did not deny stealing the money. At least he must have been in this house when Old Soc heard him speak. It was very—

Anne's eyelids closed and she dropped off to sleep.

She was awakened by a raised voice. This time the room was flooded with light and the voice was Dodge's, shouting outside the house. He had discovered the torn ivy and he was furious. Anne slipped out of bed and unlocked her door. She did not want the staff to know of the way she barricaded herself at night.

When the maid tapped at the door and came in with the breakfast tray, Anne was already dressed and ready for the day. "Good morning," she said cheerfully, as though she had not spent a night broken by terror. "Put the tray on the table in my workroom, will you, please?"

She took a final look at herself in the mirror, at the powder-blue tweed suit, the dainty white blouse with a tiny ruff encircling her neck, making her look as young as Sharon.

"You are up early, Miss Kendrick."

"Someone was shouting. It woke me."

"That was Mr. Dodge, Miss. Carrying on like mad. Someone tore down part of the vine along the side of the house last night." The maid lowered her voice to conspiratorial tones and looked cautiously over her shoulder. "I wasn't supposed to tell—he doesn't want the servants to get upset—but I'm sure he thinks it was a burglar."

"In that case he should have called the state police. I'll speak to him about it."

"Oh, please, Miss Kendrick." The frightened maid clasped her hands. "Please," she implored, "don't say anything. Mr. Dodge is in an awful temper. His face is all the colors of the rainbow from that bruise and Mrs. Dodge is sick—she's staying in bed today. He's just beside himself. He'll fire me."

"I'll see that you aren't fired," Anne assured her.

"Thanks a lot. But even if I stayed on he'd take it out of me. I know what he's like."

"All right. I'll let it go this time," Anne promised.

Later, as she was running down the stairs, Dodge met her. The bruise, as the maid had said, was all the colors of the rainbow and not one of them was becoming to him. His manner was stiffer, more dignified than ever, to counteract the ludicrous effect of his swollen, discolored cheek and the eye which had practically disappeared from view.

"A telephone call for you, Miss Kendrick."

Anne stifled a desire to giggle as she looked at him but she managed to control it.

"Thank you, Dodge. Who is calling?"

"He refused to say, Miss." Dodge could not conceal his sense of outraged dignity at this.

The voice at the other end of the telephone said, "Good morning, Miss Kendrick. This is Tim Marston—please," he added quickly before she could speak, "don't mention my name. Something rather serious has come up and I'd like to discuss it with you. As I can't leave the drugstore—there is no one else to fill prescriptions and there might be an emergency call, you know—"

"I quite understand," Anne said.

"Would it be frightfully inconvenient for you to come here?"

"Of course not," Anne said. "I'll do that."

"That's fine," he said heartily.

Dodge was hovering around within earshot. Anne smiled mischievously to herself. Let him make something out of that conversation if he could!

"I'm going out for a drive," she told him. "I'll be back for lunch at the usual time."

"Thank you, Miss." He opened the front door. His curiosity got the better of him. "I hope it wasn't bad news."

"Oh, not at all," she said breezily. "Speaking of bad news, I'm sorry to hear Mrs. Dodge is not well."

He stiffened. "Thank you. She'll be all right with a day's rest. She has already planned the menus with the cook."

Anne drove cautiously along the mountain road. Ten days ago she had come this way for the first time. She slowed for a curve. Here she had nearly run into the Park Department truck and Griff Trent had scolded her. Scolded her because he was frightened for her safety.

If I had known then what I was heading into, Anne thought, I don't believe I'd have had the courage to enter that house. I'd have turned and run.

Her chin went up. I won't turn and I won't run. I'll—

I'll keep swinging. What is that line? "Cowards die many times before their deaths."

The drugstore was empty when Anne entered. Behind a partition came a clatter of dishes as Stella cleared up from the breakfast rush. Then the door to the office opened and Tim Marston looked out. He smiled at Anne, glanced cautiously toward the partition, and beckoned to her.

When Anne had entered the office he closed the door, shook hands warmly, and pulled up a chair for her. "Thank you for coming," he said.

"You made me so curious that nothing could have kept me away," Anne declared.

"Nice to see you smile like that. When I saw you drive up, I thought you were about ready to cry on my shoulder."

"That photographic eye I've heard about," Anne laughed.

"That photographic eye is my reason for calling you," the druggist said. "I have a flair for remembering faces. Once I have seen a person his or her face is recorded in my memory as clearly as a snapshot pasted into an album. I don't forget it. Well, Miss Kendrick, this week I have been seeing some faces around this town that I once saw under very different circumstances."

She looked an eager question.

"Some of Uncle Sam's boys heard about this photographic eye of mine and they smuggled me into several big Communist meetings. They wanted me to get a look at as many people as possible. In a small way it is my war work—or I'd rather think of it as my work for peace. All they wanted me to do was to remember those faces and be on the lookout if they should turn up again anywhere."

"Go on," Anne begged him. "I can't wait."

"Three of them, two women and a man, appeared in the village several days ago. I began to ask some discreet questions here and there and discovered—" he peered at her gravely over his spectacles—"that they were making arrangements to buy some of your property, Miss Kendrick."

Anne's handbag fell with a clatter to the floor and she bent over to pick it up.

"My property! Communists! But that's impossible."

"I'm afraid not," he told her gravely.

"But why would Communists want to move here?"

"The military base, for one thing. Any number of reasons."

Angry spots of color burned on Anne's cheeks. "May I use your telephone, Mr. Marston?" she asked crisply.

As she got Gaston Cosgrove's number the druggist studied her. She was under some sort of strain, he thought. There was too much tension in the slim body, her eyes were too bright.

Something was worrying her. He reproached himself for having neglected to see whether she was getting along all right. It was a big adjustment for any girl to make, coming without warning into the responsibilities of a large fortune.

Plenty of character there, he decided. A good brain and a fine sense of integrity. But the sunniness of nature that had so won him at first sight was clouded over.

"Mr. Cosgrove," he heard her say, "this is Anne Kendrick."

The lawyer's voice was so clear that Marston could hear it across the desk.

"I was planning to call you a little later, Miss Kendrick," Cosgrove said. "I just got back from New York. And I have grand news. I've sold five pieces of property. All at top prices. All ready for signing on the dotted line. Probably have the whole thing cleared up by tomorrow. What do you think of that?" His voice rang out triumphantly.

"I'm afraid those sales can't go through, Mr. Cosgrove."

"What!" he spluttered. "What's that?"

"I want to see you before you do anything further about selling my property."

"But I tell you the deal's closed," he said impatiently. "It's too late. They're coming in today."

"I won't sell the property, Mr. Cosgrove!" Anne's tone ended the discussion.

"Wait a minute! Not so fast, young lady. We can't treat people that way. Once a deal is made—as long as I am handling the property for you—"

"That's just it," Anne said. "I don't intend to sell. That's final. If you don't care to do business my way—"

"You will take it out of my hands?" Over the phone Anne could hear Cosgrove's heavy breathing. "You win, Miss Kendrick. But may I ask why you are taking this extraordinary stand? Why, without any warning—?"

"There is no time for a warning if the sale is to go through right away," she pointed out.

"What is your objection to selling?"

"I've just discovered that the prospective buyers are Communists."

"What!" This time it was a yell.

Anne pulled the receiver hastily away from her ear. She could hear the clack-clack-clack of his voice. When it quieted down she put the receiver back.

"Where did you hear that cockeyed story?" he was saying.

Marston shook his head warningly.

"I am sorry. I heard it in confidence."

Marston scrawled something on a piece of paper and shoved

it across the desk to Anne. She read it and nodded. With her eyes on it she asked, "How did you meet these people, Mr. Cosgrove?"

"Through a man staying at the Inn here. Seems to be a nice fellow. Ned Crane—oh, you know him, don't you?"

"Ned Crane!" Anne gasped.

"I'll put these people off," Cosgrove said, "some way or other. Though it will be embarrassing. I'd like to talk to you later."

"Come for tea this afternoon," Anne suggested.

"I wish I could but I have a number of appointments."

"Then make it dinner at seven."

"That will be swell. We'll thrash it all out and get things cleared up between us." His voice was hearty with bluff friendliness, as though he had not run an emotional gamut from shocked surprise to anger to startled protest to submission to defeat.

"Well!" Anne expelled a long breath as she put down the telephone. She remembered Joe Bennet saying, "Watch out for Cosgrove. He's tricky about human relations."

Tricky? He had sounded genuinely shocked. Naturally he was upset at her threat of transferring her business. The loss of a big estate would be a serious matter for him. She hoped it would not be necessary.

She looked up to find Marston's keen eyes on her face.

"Photographing me for your memory book?" she asked gaily.

"One of my pleasantest pictures," he said with a smile. "And I begin to see why Mrs. Williams felt so safe in leaving her property in your hands. That was dealt with as decisively as though you were a real businessman, Miss Kendrick. I'm proud of you."

"Thank you kindly, sir, she said." Anne laughed but her eyes were wet from his unexpected sympathy, from fatigue growing out of sleepless, watchful nights, from the fears that hovered over her as darkness fell in the evenings, from her lack of anyone to talk to.

She held her lids wide open, trying to keep back the tears. It would be embarrassing to break down in front of a man whom she barely knew.

"Is something worrying you?" he asked gently.

"Yes, but I can't—I'd like to tell you later when I—" She broke off, her lips trembling.

He nodded understandingly and escorted her to the door. He half opened it and then turned back to her.

"What do you know about this man Crane, Miss Kendrick?"

"Nothing good," Anne said.

There was an edge on his voice. "I think we'll have to look into Mr. Crane's background. At once."

"As long as you just make him go away," Anne said fervently.

She walked out into the drugstore. Sharon Ames, in a russet sweater and matching plaid skirt, was at the soda fountain, finishing a dish of ice cream.

She whirled around, her face flushed.

"You're mean to Ned Crane!" she cried. "I heard you, Anne Kendrick. Trying to get Mr. Marston to drive him away. You're unfair, all of you. You're just jealous. He's not going to be driven away—not by anyone. Period."

"Sharon," Anne said gently, "you don't understand—"

"I understand plenty," the younger girl said stormily. "You're all ganging up on Ned. Well, all I've got to say is —you'll be sorry."

With a whirl of russet skirts she ran out of the drugstore, banging the door behind her.

"Dear me," Marston said mildly, though his eyes twinkled. "I'm afraid the Trents have been spoiling that young niece of theirs."

The door opened and a thin, dark-haired young man came into the drugstore.

"Hello, Pedro," Marston said. "You still around?"

"Hi, there," Pedro answered. He looked curiously at Anne and then strolled over to the cigarette counter.

Anne shook hands with Marston and went out. She drove slowly through the village before returning home, in the hope that she might find Sharon, especially as the sky threatened rain. But the girl had vanished.

One minute more and I'd have poured out all my worries, Anne thought. And made a spectacle of myself by bursting into tears. This last problem is just too much. Ned Crane bringing in Communists to buy my property. And Sharon defending him.

She left the car to be put away and went up the steps. One of the maids opened the door for her. Dodge, who was talking softly over the telephone, finished his conversation in a hurry as she appeared.

"Mr. Cosgrove will be here for dinner, Dodge," she said before she went upstairs.

Today there was no need for the ambulance and time hung heavy on her hands. She looked out at the tiny torrents of rain that ran above the window. The mountain was shrouded in fog. A mist lay over the valley.

Among Mrs. Williams's books Anne found an autographed

copy of Jimmy Williams's poems. She tried to read but so many unanswered questions hammered at her mind that she could not do it. On impulse she went into the nurse-companion's rooms, looking for a trace of the woman whose sobbing she had heard the night before. There was the print of a body on the spread, the pillowcase was dented where the unknown woman had flung herself in a paroxysm of grief or despair.

Who was she? How had she entered a locked house? Certainly not up the vine, the way the man had come.

As Anne wandered through the house she switched on lights in all the rooms, trying to dispel the twilight gloom that filled them, to drive out the shadows.

At last her conscience troubled her. I really ought to ask how Mrs. Dodge is feeling, she thought, and she went to the Dodges' apartment on the third floor. The door to their living room was open and there were voices talking eagerly. Anne would have hesitated but she recognized them both. One was the harsh voice with its hissing s's which belonged to Mrs. Dodge. The other, low-pitched and musical, was the voice of the woman who had cried in the night.

Without hesitation Anne opened the door and went in.

XVI

MRS. DODGE was sitting in an armchair, dressed in black wool with a small white collar, her hair pulled back in its usual uncompromising knot. There was no sign of the illness that was supposed to have put her to bed. There were plenty of signs, however, that she was in a bad temper.

The other woman was a staggering contrast to the grim, elderly housekeeper. There was something exotic about her. She seemed to be in her middle twenties, her blond hair had been arranged by an expert in a deceptively simple style, her eyebrows were lengthened until they reached the temple, her eyelids were shadowed with blue, artificial lashes that seemed as extravagant as the four-inch diamond earrings that swung and glittered as she turned her head. The room was filled with the expensive scent she wore.

Apparently she felt very much at home in the housekeeper's room because she was lying on a couch, wearing a rose velvet negligee that was cut low, generously revealing her white arms and shoulders. Her mouth, heavily rouged, was sulky. To Anne's surprise, she seemed to be intimidated by the housekeeper.

As Anne appeared in the doorway the conversation broke off abruptly. Mrs. Dodge, her mouth opening and shutting like a fish out of water, slowly got to her feet, one hand nervously smoothing her skirt. The blond woman, moving with lovely grace, sat up. Instinctively her hands moved up and covered the earrings.

The awkward pause lengthened.

"Do you want something, Miss Kendrick?" the housekeeper asked at last. "If you had rung—"

"I came to inquire about you," Anne said. "Dodge told me you weren't well, that you were staying in bed today."

Mrs. Dodge looked from Anne to the woman in the rose velvet negligee. With a swift gesture the latter dropped her hands. The earrings had disappeared. Then she said, with a touch of defiance, "You might as well tell her."

The nervous smoothing of the skirt continued in a helpless sort of indecision. Then Mrs. Dodge said, "Miss Kendrick, this is my daughter Minna, who has come to visit me."

Anne looked in surprise at the exotic creature. The Dodges' daughter? She smiled. "How do you do, Miss Dodge."

"Not Miss Dodge," the blond woman said. "I am Mrs. Jimmy Williams."

"Minna, you fool!" It was Dodge's furious voice behind Anne. Then his face was blank and still—and watchful.

Ugh, Anne thought, he is like one of those snakes I saw at the Bronx Zoo. Only there isn't any nice thick glass partition between us in case he strikes.

Minna shrugged her bare white shoulders. "It had to come out some time or other," she said. "Anyhow," she told Anne, "it hasn't been fair to Jimmy. He would have hated this, knowing that I was keeping still about our marriage, as though I was ashamed of it. When I was so proud of him!" She threw back her head. "I want the whole world to know I was his wife."

Minna Dodge! Jimmy Williams's widow! Anne felt as though her head were reeling. Was this why the Dodges had hated her, why they had tried to drive her away from Mountain Lodge? Her mind was a blur of mixed-up pictures: the woman crying in the night, the man who threatened her, who talked of blackmail—

"Of course you want people to know you are married," she said steadily. "Why didn't you announce it before?"

Minna told her the same story she had told Griff. "I was so confused," she went on. "I didn't know what was best—for Jimmy or for Mrs. Williams."

Anne sat down in the chair Dodge held for her, not because she wanted to stay but because her knees had given way under her. Instinct told her that something was wrong, that there was no real grief behind Minna's words. Just a watchful sort of bravado. Would she have revealed her position if Anne had not caught her in her mother's sitting room?

"I wish you had known Jimmy," Minna said softly. "He was so gay and he was a fine poet too."

"How long were you married before he died?"

"Two years."

Anne remembered the book of poems she had been reading. It had been published three months before his death. She recalled the sonnet sequence, the line, "Hair dark as midnight." Written for the blond Minna? And the couplet that ended the leading poem:

> If I must end, let it not be at night,
> But, like a singing lark, upon the flight.

She repeated the lines softly. Minna's eyes were blank. Anne's heart missed a beat. Minna hadn't recognized the lines! What did that mean? That she had never read a word of the poetry of the man she claimed to have loved? That simply was not possible.

Minna realized that in some way she had blundered. "Mrs. Williams believed me," she said. "She promised me Jimmy's insurance. She took the money out of the bank. Only—"

"Only someone stole it," Anne said. Should she mention the man who had taken it? Better not until she had talked to Cosgrove.

It was Mrs. Dodge who said, "I was wondering, Miss Kendrick—as long as Mrs. Williams wanted Minna to have the money—her own husband's insurance—and it wouldn't mean much to you—"

"I'll have to ask my lawyer," Anne said. "He is dining with me tonight. I'll get his opinion. Of course, he'll want to see some proof of the marriage."

"But I've already explained, I left my marriage certificate with Mrs. Williams. And no one has been able to find it. It has disappeared."

Anne got up. "Mr. Cosgrove will probably get in touch with you." At the doorway she stopped. "By the way, Dodge, someone broke into the house last night."

The words were like a bombshell in the room. Mrs. Dodge drew in her breath like a hissing snake. Dodge stiffened.

"Perhaps," Minna said breathlessly, "you heard me. I arrived unexpectedly and my father let me in."

"It wasn't you I saw," Anne said, "unless you climbed up the ivy."

"Saw!" Minna was chalk-white.

"There was a man on the ivy. I saw him from my window."

"Did you—see him—clearly?" Minna got out the words jerkily.

I won't say there is nothing I could recognize except for a watch dial with long modernistic numbers, Anne thought.

"I might be able to identify him," she said vaguely. "I suppose you reported the housebreaking to the police, Dodge."

For once the butler was ill-at-ease, on the defensive "I saw the broken vine but nothing was missing. I thought perhaps the storm had done it."

Anne nodded. "I'm glad to see you have recovered, Mrs. Dodge. Good morning—Mrs. Williams."

That afternoon the storm broke. The world outside the house was blotted out. The rain beat angry fingers against the windows, the force of the wind made the house shake.

Anne changed to a black satin damask skirt and a short emerald velvet jacket for dinner. In spite of the storm, Gaston Cosgrove arrived promptly at seven.

The white hair above his youthful face was wet with rain. He shook hands with her heartily as though no hasty words had passed between them that morning. Then he stretched out his hands to the crackling fire.

"This feels good!" he exclaimed. "We have some bad storms up here but this is really a corker. And what a ride! My car stalled several times coming up the mountain road and the wind nearly blew me off on one of the curves. Heaven help the sailors on a night like this!"

He turned around to face her. "You are terrific tonight! Emerald is the right color for you. Guess I haven't seen a color that isn't right for you."

Anne laughed and dropped him a mock curtsy.

"Well, young lady, you gave me quite a shock this morning."

Dodge stood in the doorway. "Dinner is served."

"Pleasure first," Anne said. "We'll dine before we talk business."

"Suits me."

The dinner table with its candles, its epergne surrounded by autumn leaves, was gay with color and helped to counteract the storm that raged over the mountain.

The dinner was delicious and the service was expert. Dodge was assisted by Della, who moved as though she were afraid of him. Anne was glad she had forbidden any business talk at the table, with Dodge hovering in the background, his ears twitching. The danger signal.

Gaston Cosgrove was at his best and his most entertaining.

He told her amusing anecdotes about Mrs. Williams, the high-handed way in which she had dealt with people who imposed on her, and her unpublicized generosity.

"She was highly intelligent," he said, "and took a great interest in public affairs, particularly in local politics."

"She must be greatly missed."

"She is. By me especially. Not only because she was a grand person and one of my closest friends but for purely selfish reasons. If she had lived she would have been of incalculable help in my campaign for political office."

He helped himself liberally to the veal scallopini and the asparagus hollandaise. "I am not," he went on, "inclined to be envious, but if I could envy anyone it would be Griffith Trent. Not," he added in a tone of contempt, "for anything he is in himself, but because of his sister. No one realizes how much he owes to the heavy financial backing and political astuteness of Clarissa Trent. With that combination behind him a man would be almost unbeatable. It makes the competition tough for the man who hasn't the same kind of backing."

Something about the pause that followed this statement made Anne wonder whether her lawyer was hoping that she would put some money into his campaign as, he implied, Mrs. Williams would have done.

To break the silence she said, "We'll have coffee in the game room, Dodge."

When Dodge had taken away the coffee tray and Cosgrove had lighted a cigarette, after offering one to Anne, which she refused, he began, "Now then—"

Anne felt her hands gripping together nervously. Then she made herself relax, straightened her shoulders, and planted the slim feet firmly on the floor.

"You have caused me a lot of trouble, young lady," Cosgrove said, "with that brain wave of yours. I had checked in New York on the financial standing of those people who wanted to buy property and they are A-1, let me tell you. Then when they came in to sign on the dotted line and make out their checks I had to fool around, postpone it, put them off with a lot of vague excuses—"

"Put them off!" Anne exclaimed. "But I told you over the telephone I didn't want to sell."

"Where did you get that wild Communist theory?"

"I'm sorry. I can't tell you that. It was revealed to me in strict confidence."

Cosgrove shrugged. "You know, Miss Kendrick," he said reasonably, "a lawyer is accustomed to working with evidence —the kind you can take into court—not sheer hearsay."

"I understand that. Please believe me when I say the information I have is more than hearsay. It is absolutely reliable."

Cosgrove gave up with a good grace. "Then I guess I made a blunder. I was too eager to sell your property for you at a good price. This man Crane who introduced them—you remember how he came to our table at the country club—you introduced us, as a matter of fact. He seems to be all right. He knows the best people around here. Including Clarissa Trent, with whom he was dancing and—your fiancé."

"My fiancé!" Anne exclaimed.

Cosgrove's eyebrows shot up. "Excuse me if I've put my foot in it. I took for granted Griffith Trent was the man Mrs. Williams intended you to marry. Just another thing that was done without consulting me."

This time he could not keep the resentment out of his voice.

"Where did you hear about that?" Anne asked.

"I don't remember. It seems to be a general rumor."

But how could it be? Anne thought. She had obeyed that crazy impulse to speak of her imaginary fiancé in the presence of four people: the Trents, Ned Crane, and Dodge. It must be Ned Crane who had spoken of it. Surely Griff Trent wouldn't—anyhow, he had refused to marry her, according to Cosgrove. Glory, how had she got herself into such a mess?

How maddening, she thought, that I can't explain that so-called fiancé of mine was just a brain storm. But so long as Ned Crane is around—it can't be long now. Tim Marston indicated that something will be done and done soon. It can't be too soon to suit me.

"Mr. Crane may not continue to know the 'best people' as long as he expects," she said crisply. "And meanwhile, please make it clear that my property is not for sale."

"You're the boss," Cosgrove said. "That reminds me—we were both a bit upset when we talked over the telephone this morning. I hope you weren't serious when you spoke of taking the management of your property out of my hands."

"As long as we understand each other on basic policies I don't see why we should not continue as we are," Anne said.

"That's fine! I know Mrs. Williams would have felt badly to have me—ousted, when she trusted me so completely."

"That reminds me," Anne said, "did Mrs. Williams ever ask you to hire a detective for her?"

"A detective?" Cosgrove echoed blankly. "Certainly not. What made you think of that?"

Anne told him of the memorandum she had found. "Wait," she said, "I'll show it to you."

She ran up to her workroom and unlocked the file in which she had placed it.

When she returned to the game room she handed it to Cosgrove. "'Ask G.C. to hire detective to check.' That's Mrs. Williams's handwriting," he said. "G.C. must refer to me.

How curious. She never mentioned such a thing to me. This may be something she wrote long ago and then forgot."

"No, I asked the chambermaid. The note was in the pocket of the dress she was wearing when she died. What did she die of, Mr. Cosgrove?"

"A heart attack," he said absently, his attention still on the memorandum, his brows drawn together together in a puzzled frown. "Now what on earth—"

"I think I know what was troubling her," Anne said. "Minna Dodge came up here several days before Mrs. Williams died to say she was Jimmy Williams's widow. She is in the house now. She just told me herself. She says she came to ask for Jimmy's insurance—"

Cosgrove's expression cleared. "By Jove, I believe that's it! That explains the money she withdrew from the bank." He nodded his head. "Yes, sir, that clears up a lot of things. I'm not surprised, you know. Jimmy was crazy about the girl. I always thought he wanted to marry her. The last time he was home on leave he dropped some hints to me—of course, I had no idea then what he was getting at—asking me to look out for his interests. I remember hearing him say, 'A guy fighting for his country doesn't accumulate much money, even for those he loves.' Then he died for his country."

"Then you feel sure he really married her?"

Cosgrove smiled. "You'll never make a lawyer, Miss Kendrick. Of course, I would want proof."

Anne told him Minna's story. "I don't believe Mrs. Williams was sure. If she had lived I think she would have hired a detective to check up on the marriage. Anyhow, Mrs. Dodge suggested that I give Minna the ten thousand dollars. I said I would consult you about it."

"Quite proper," he beamed. "Mrs. Williams obviously intended to do so. But I would like to talk to the girl first."

"I'll send for her. But there is something else I want to tell you."

She described the conversation she had overhead in the night between Minna and an unknown man who apparently had taken the ten thousand dollars and claimed to know all about the missing will. She told how Minna had cried out, "Blackmail," and how she had sobbed after the man was gone.

"So she knows who took the money," Cosgrove said grimly.

"And so does Dodge! I'm sure it is the same man who followed me from the Trents'. I sent Dodge out to investigate and he came back with that black eye you noticed at dinner and in a flaming temper. He knew who hit him, I'm sure of it."

Cosgrove got to his feet. "All this sounds pretty queer to

me. I'm going to investigate thoroughly before giving you any advice. And tomorrow I'll have a talk with Minna Dodge or Williams or whoever she is. Sorry to leave so early but I have a political meeting scheduled—if anyone will come out on a night like this."

He gave Dodge a searching look as the latter helped him into his topcoat and then, with a wave of the hand to Anne, he went out into the downpour, running for his car.

Dodge closed the door behind him and answered the telephone.

"Washington is calling you, Miss Kendrick."

"Anne," said Griffith Trent's voice. "Anne, are you all right?"

"Of course I am."

"I can tell by that lilt in your voice. I just wanted to say things are clearing up here sooner than we expected. I'll be back in a day or two."

He laughed softly. "Have you missed me a little bit?"

XVII

THE STORM continued all the following day, accompanied by sleet, making the mountain road so dangerous that Anne stayed home, unable to settle down to anything.

There were some minor incidents to break the monotony. The pleasantest of these was a phone call from Rissa Trent, saying that Griff would be back the next day—the date for the reception in Anne's honor.

"It sounds out of this world!" Anne exclaimed. "I can't tell you how much I appreciate the way you are trying to make me welcome here."

"Heavens, we are the grateful ones! It's a joy to have someone like you at Mountain Lodge. And I'm not the only one who thinks so, either."

Anne put down the telephone with a warm glow in her heart. Making friends was always a delight. But especially so with Rissa Trent. She had a great deal of her brother's charm.

No use deceiving myself, Anne thought. Whenever I think of Griffith Trent, the steadiness in his eyes, the laughter in his voice, his quiet dependability, my heart turns over.

Forget it. Never let him suspect how you feel. He refused to marry you once. He's a woman-hater since Zoe

Mason jilted him. Then why did he ask me over the phone, "Have you missed me a little bit?" I nearly told him how much.

Why can't I put him out of my mind? I'm the career gal who only a few weeks ago was going to do big things in television. Remember? And now all I hear is a little voice saying a woman's best career is marriage.

I mustn't dwell on it any more. Griffith Trent is not for me. Be careful when you meet him at Rissa's party tomorrow, Anne Kendrick. Don't be too glad to see him.

At her workroom desk Anne caught up with her correspondence, trying to sound gay and happy in her letters to her old friends, to give no hint of the troubles she had encountered at Mountain Lodge.

One letter from an acquaintance at the television station was more difficult to answer.

"What goes on up there, Anne?" the friend had written. "Are the wedding bells to ring soon? The columnists seem to know more about your activities than your friends do. See the attached and watch your step."

The "attached" was a clipping from a popular newspaper column:

A certain good-looking man about town is missing from Gotham these days. The grapevine reports he has followed a young lady whose charm and singing voice are well known to the owners of TV sets. To her attractions has just been added a large fortune. Good hunting.

Anne was enraged. She read the malicious clipping, her cheeks flaming. Everyone would see it. At least she could stop one speculation about it quickly.

"I hope you aren't taking that paragraph in the column seriously," she wrote. "Ned Crane did come up here but there will be no wedding bells."

The thought of that news item made her furious when she thought of it. She remembered a precept her father had often quoted to her: "God grant me serenity to accept the things I cannot change, courage to change the things I can, and wisdom to know the difference."

That at least she could change. Any rumors that connected her name with Ned Crane's she could scotch.

She was interrupted by the sound of Dodge's raised voice. "Miss Kendrick won't see you. Get out now without making any trouble."

"I won't go," said a voice that was vaguely familiar, "until you tell her I'm here. I know she'll see me."

"What is your business?"

"Tell her it's about the parrot."

Anne ran to the head of the stairs. "Tell him I'll see him," she called.

Dodge, his raised eyebrows expressing disapproval, stood back and let Jake Wingate enter the hall, where he stood dripping on the floor, the rain pouring off his waterproof coat.

Anne came down the stairs, told Dodge to take the wet coat, which he did grudgingly, and led the farmer into the game room.

He stood awkwardly in front of the fire, his wet clothes steaming, looking around him.

"Gee, this is quite a place!"

"Tell me, Jake," Anne said eagerly, "do you know anything about the parrot?"

"Well," he said slowly, with a farmer's caution, "I do and I don't. But like my wife said, what did we have to lose but a trip in the rain, and maybe five hundred dollars to gain."

Anne controlled her breathless impatience. The more Jake was hurried the longer it would take him to talk.

At her suggestion he sat uneasily on the edge of a chair and tried unsuccessfully to hide his muddy boots under it.

"Well," the farmer went on in his leisurely way, "I was over to the garridge and machine shop where they are repairing my tractor and I heard a yawping sound that was kinda familiar. I sort of moseyed around a bit and in an open window of the apartment over the shop I saw the cage and a gray parrot. Looked like the same one to me."

Jake looked sadly at the mud on the carpet. "I've sure messed things up. My wife would give me a raking over the coals if she saw what I done."

"That's all right," Anne assured him. "No harm done. Did you ask about the parrot?"

"No, ma'am. If someone was hiding it, I figured there was no use letting them get wise that I was on to where it was. But I asked, casual like, if the mechanic lived over the shop. Convenient place for him, I said. So he said no, he was renting it for a spell to a guy with a foreign name."

The farmer fumbled in his pocket. "I'm not so good at names. Especially foreign ones. I wrote it down. Yup, here it is." He spread out the grimy piece of paper slowly, put on his glasses and cleared his throat, while Anne was nearly frantic with impatience. "Yup, this is it. Pedro Brocchi. He's the one who's got your bird. Anyways, it's a gray parrot and I've never seen another one anywheres."

"Thanks a lot." Anne shook hands with him. "Don't mention this to anyone, will you?"

"Not a soul," Jake promised. "But you won't forget us for the reward if it *is* your bird?"

"You can count on me," Anne promised.

Unexpectedly Jake smiled. "I guess your word's good enough for me," he said. "I always figure I know a lot about human nature. Pretty hard to fool me on that. You're the kind whose word is as good as his bond."

Before Anne could call Cosgrove to report on the whereabouts of the missing parrot, the lawyer called her. His voice was grave.

"Miss Kendrick, there are some very unexpected new developments. Grave developments. It will take a few days to check on them. Then we must have a conference."

"Have you seen—" she hesitated to mention Minna's name because Dodge always hovered around within earshot when she talked over the telephone.

"Yes, I've had a talk with her. Something has come up—something totally unexpected—a considerable shock to me. But I don't want to alarm you. After all, it may be a tempest in a teapot. I hope so for your sake."

"I haven't the slightest idea what you are talking about," Anne declared.

"Well, we'll get together before the week is out. Meanwhile, I'll be seeing you at the big shindig at Forest Edge tomorrow."

He hung up before Anne could report to him about Old Soc. What on earth did it mean? The lawyer sounded terribly upset. Alarm me? What about? Surely those Communists can't make any trouble now they have been found out. Or is Ned Crane up to something else? Perhaps Mr. Marston has already got rid of him in some way. Strange how one human being can poison everything he touches, hurt everyone he meets. Ned hurt Rissa, he nearly hurt me, he may hurt Sharon unless we protect her. He got Mr. Cosgrove into trouble by introducing him to those Communists. Why must there be such people to dim the radiance of the world?

Next day it seemed to Anne that nothing could dim the radiance of the world. Glorious was the word for that day. The sky was an inverted bowl of lapis lazuli. Sunlight caught new colors in woods and fields. Now that the big autumn show of leaves was almost over, bushes and tree trunks, ground and stubble, revealed softer, more muted brown and russet and gold. Against the brilliant blue of the sky the trunks of trees seemed almost black. Everything was in clearer, sharper outline.

The bare branches of trees made the world seem wider, freer, more spacious. And underfoot was a soft, springy carpet of leaves like a magnificent Persian carpet, that made Anne feel as though she were walking on air.

Or was she particularly happy for some other reason? Some reason she would not acknowledge to herself? Could be, she admitted. She took a final look in the mirror. She wore moss-green brocaded in gold, ballet length. I'm glad I wore my mother's diamonds in the long earrings. If I do say so, they are becoming. And that new hair-do, short and waved smooth to my head. Somehow it makes my hair seem blonder than ever before. Honey-blond. Not bad, my girl. The corsage of white orchids from Rissa and Griff completes the picture.

From the moment when she arrived at Forest Edge she knew that the Trent reception in her honor was going to be a grand party.

Rissa Trent, in a charming blue frock with a double string of real pearls, came to meet her.

"Welcome, Glamour Girl," she said. "Heavens, you are going to be a sensation, Anne! Stand next to me in the line, will you, so that I can present your future neighbors and friends?"

The next hour was a succession of handshakes, of laughing comments, of words of welcome that sounded warm and genuine. For the first time Anne felt that she was accepted as a permanent part of the community, that her new neighbors wanted her to feel that she belonged among them.

There were too many new faces for her to be able to remember them all. Some she remembered without difficulty.

First was Griff, looking as smooth, smiling and rested as though he had not just flown back from a strenuous night battle before the adjournment of Congress.

He held her hand in his warm grasp and looked earnestly down into her face. Then his own fine face lighted up in a smile.

"Now that I see you looking so radiant I can't imagine what I have been worrying about."

"Thank you for the orchids. They are really fabulous."

"Thank you for wearing them," he said soberly. Then his eyes twinkled. "By the way, you didn't answer my question last night."

To Anne's relief Rissa whispered, "Move on, Griff. Go entertain your other guests. You mustn't monopolize the guest of honor."

"First dance?" Griff asked and Anne nodded. She tugged at the hand which he had been holding all this time and he released it at once. "See you later for a real talk," he said. "Oh, before Rissa drives me into outer darkness, Miss Kendrick, let me present a colleague of mine in the House, Mr. John Clinton."

Anne smiled at Clinton. He was a grand-looking person with the noble-Roman type of face but without the stuffed-shirt quality that sometimes goes with it. Clinton, however, after a few pleasant words turned eagerly from Anne to his hostess. Now I wonder, Anne thought to herself. It would be fine if a splendid person like Rissa can fall in love with someone who would make up to her for that disastrous experience with Ned Crane.

Sharon Ames, in an aqua net frock, was flitting around, looking very pretty and imitating the graciousness of her aunt. Except when she had to greet Anne. Her manner was so stiff, so obviously hostile, that Rissa was taken aback.

"Sharon," she warned her in a low tone.

"I'll be polite, but I don't have to pretend to *like* her, for Pete's sake," Sharon muttered.

Rissa threw a look of consternation and apology at Anne when Sharon had gone off.

"I'm horribly sorry. I don't know what makes her act like that."

"I do," Anne said softly. "Look."

They watched Sharon skimming across the room, throwing gay nods and greetings to right and left, but hurrying as quickly as she could to Ned Crane, who leaned against a mantel massed with flowers.

Tall and good-looking, his blond hair sleek and smooth, thumb and forefinger stroking his small mustache, he watched her come, his eyes holding the laughing welcome so familiar to both Rissa and Anne.

As Sharon reached his side breathlessly, he tucked her hand under his arm, murmuring something complimentary that sent color into her cheeks, and sauntered away from the crowd with her.

Between smiling introductions, Rissa explained *sotto voce* to Anne: "You already know Parson Savage, Anne."

"How do you do, my dear. You look ravishing in that frock."

(*"Anne, I didn't ask Ned!"*)

"Miss Kendrick, some neighbors from that lovely estate in the valley."

"We've been looking forward to having such an attractive person in our neighborhood."

(*"Sharon must have sent him an invitation."*)

"Mr. Cosgrove." No trace in Rissa's manner of her opinion of the man who was running against her brother. "How nice of you to come."

"Miss Kendrick, you get lovelier each time we meet," the

lawyer said. He looked around and lowered his voice. "This ought to pile up the votes for Congressman Trent," he told her bitterly. "I can't hope to beat this." He moved on rapidly as though afraid Anne might question him about his telephone call.

("Anne, what shall I do about Ned Crane?")

Anne was too happy to worry. She giggled. "Why don't you ask Griff to throw him over the wall?"

"What!" After her startled exclamation Rissa burst into a gale of laughter.

"What's the joke, Rissa? Let me in on it too." Zoe Mason in a sheathlike black dress with an enormous cartwheel hat of gold velvet was smiling at her hostess.

"Just a ridiculous comment of Anne Kendrick's," Rissa said.

Rissa nodded coolly to Anne. "You're quite a famous girl. I saw a mention of you in the paper the other day. Who's the lucky man about town?"

As the orchestra began to play softly on the terrace she said, "Yummy! My favorite tune. Where's Griff? . . . There you are, darling. Dance this with me?"

"First dance with the guest of honor," Griff said. "Keep one for me later, Zoe."

He led Anne toward the terrace, slipped his arm around her and they moved off in perfect step. The flowers, the tantalizing music, the friendly faces, Griff's arms holding her gently but firmly—it was too much, too much happiness for one person.

Across her mind, unsought, came the memory of grim headlines, newsreel pictures. On the other side of the world young men were fighting, were dying. Joe Bennet, warm-hearted and gay of spirit, was not here because he had reported to the Marines.

Griff looked down at her. "What's wrong, Sober-face?"

"Thinking about Joe and the war."

"Forget it for now."

"I will."

"You still haven't answered my question," he teased her. "Did you miss me a little bit?"

"A lot of things have been happening," she said hastily, to sidetrack him. "I've got a lot to tell you."

"I'll take you home later. We can talk then. All right?"

She nodded. Beside her there was a ripple of excited laughter. Seeing the set look on Griff's face she knew before she looked around that Sharon was dancing with Ned Crane, whose blond head was bent over her dark one while he whispered to her.

XVIII

"NO," Griff said firmly, "I'm not going to walk you home through the woods. Not in those silver slippers. The princess's chariot awaits at the door."

Through the window Anne saw the long, sleek car.

"How stunning! Like a greyhound, ready to dash away. I'll bet it does a million miles an hour."

"It won't," Griff told her. "Not on these mountain roads where anything can happen and practically everything does."

He waited until Anne had gone for her coat and then he turned to Rissa.

"I'm glad you're taking Anne home," she said. "Ever since that man chased her through the woods I've been worried."

"So have I," he said gruffly.

"What do you think is wrong, Griff?"

"I don't know. Could be Aunt Mayme made enemies who have transferred their hatred to Anne. Could be someone is trying to drive her out of that house for an unknown reason."

"But can't you find out?"

"I intend to find out."

"Have you any idea what is back of all this?"

"Yes, I have, Rissa." He gave her a tabloid version of his meeting with Señorita Lola, who had turned out to be Mrs. Jimmy Williams.

"Minna and Jimmy!" Rissa exclaimed. "I simply can't understand it. But it would explain one thing that always puzzled me. Dodge made every effort to cover up Jimmy's shortcomings so Aunt Mayme wouldn't find out. If Jimmy had married Minna, naturally Dodge would want Aunt Mayme's money and property to go to them."

"But you know as well as I do, Rissa, that Jimmy could not handle money. If he had had the Williams estate it would have slipped through his fingers in a few years. Aunt Mayme knew that too. She felt responsible for what happened to it. That's why she chose Anne, because that gal has a level head and a sense of responsibility, because—what are you smiling at?" he accused her.

"You are terribly in love with Anne, aren't you, Griff?"

"No trespassing on private property, Rissa."

"I know. I shouldn't have said anything. But she's such a darling. I do hope—all right, I won't say another word."

"The first thing we've got to do," Griff said, "is to make

sure she's safe." He broke off as Anne came back wearing a short white wool jacket.

"Rissa, it was wonderful," Anne told her. "The nicest party I've ever been to and one of the happiest days of my life. How can I thank you for all that?"

"By continuing to be your own self," Rissa said.

"Amen to that," Griff declared. He offered his arm formally. "Madam, the carriage waits."

"Sir!" Anne curtsied and accepted his arm.

Griff drove in silence for a while and Anne stole quick glances at his profile. There was something strong and competent and reliable about him. For the first time since her arrival at Mountain Lodge, when she had been awakened by the voice that seemed to come from beside her bed, she felt completely safe and protected. She let out a long sigh of relief and slid down in the seat with her head resting against the back.

Before they reached her house he turned off onto a side road and switched off the motor.

"Now, Anne," he said, turning to her, "we can have a talk without any risk of Dodge overhearing us. What has been going on at Mountain Lodge?"

She sat up. "So much that I hardly know where to start." Her voice was too tight, too nervous.

He laughed, and there was warmth, tenderness and reassurance in his laughter. "Begin at the beginning and go on till you come to the end: then stop. That's been a good rule ever since the King of Hearts gave it to the White Rabbit."

Her voice was more relaxed when she spoke again. "You make me feel that everything will come out all right in the end."

His hand covered hers. "Everything *will* come out all right in the end." He cleared his voice of huskiness.

She was grateful to the darkness which concealed the warm surge of color in her face.

"Well," she began a trifle breathlessly, "first of all, I know who warned me to leave the house that first night I was there. It was Mrs. Dodge."

Griff gave a low whistle of astonishment. "All right," he admitted, "you have certainly surprised me. Somehow I never thought of a woman trying to frighten you. Rissa said something about a man who chased you through the woods."

She nodded. "And I know who it was. *And* I know who stole the parrot—and—"

"Hey," he protested, "one thing at a time. You're going too fast for me."

Anne described her realization that someone was following

103

her, seeing the illuminated watch dial with the long modernistic figures, and running. She had heard the sound of the steps pounding after her. Something of the panic she had felt then was in her voice now.

Griff released her hand and slipped his arm around her. "Steady, there," he said, his voice comforting. "You're safe now. You'll be safe from now on. That's a promise, Anne."

"Sorry," she said shakily. "I don't always act like a clinging vine." She drew herself away and Griff removed his arm.

Don't be such an idiot, she reminded herself. He is only being kind. Treating me the way he would his niece Sharon if she had been in danger. It doesn't mean a thing to him. Don't let him see how much it means to you.

"So then I sent Dodge to see if he could find out who chased me. He was gone a long time. When he came back he was so furious he could hardly speak. He said there was no one outside but, just the same, Griff, his cheek was badly bruised. He said he'd run into a tree, but I think he met the man who followed me and they fought."

"Then Dodge must know who he was."

"So do I—now. Oh, there's so much to say."

"And plenty of time to say it," he reminded her. "Go on."

"I'd better finish this part first." Anne told him about being awakened in the night, listening through the grating, and hearing the conversation in the nurse-companion's rooms between an unknown man and woman. Then seeing the man climb down the vine and recognizing the watch dial.

"The next day," she went on, "one of the maids told me Mrs. Dodge was ill and I went to see how she was. Someone was with her—her daughter Minna—"

Griff gave a low exclamation.

"And she told me she was Mrs. Jimmy Williams." Anne went on quickly with her story of the interview with the three Dodges.

"Hold it a moment, Anne. I want to get these facts clear in my mind. The man who chased you is—or was—in love with Minna. He practically confessed to stealing the ten thousand dollars and he knows—a quote—all about the mysterious missing will. Right so far?"

Anne nodded and then realized he could not see her in the dark. "That's right."

"And Minna said something about blackmail?"

"Yes."

"And Dodge sticks to his story that he did not meet anyone in the dark."

"Yes," she said again.

"And Mrs. Dodge suggests that you pay another ten thousand dollars."

When she agreed he said, "Well, I've got that much straight. I wasn't surprised to hear about Minna." He told her about the telephone call and how he and Joe Bennet had met Señorita Lola at the night club. "I've a kind of suspicion I know who the man is, Anne."

"So have I," she surprised him by saying. "I think his name is Pedro Brocchi and he has Old Soc, although he told Minna he had not stolen the parrot."

"How on earth did you find that out?"

"Jake Wingate, the farmer who found it in the first place. Joe told him about the reward and said to look for someone saying 'Smart cooky.' And Pedro does say it. I heard him myself."

"That's queer," Griff said in a puzzled tone. "Why would he admit taking the money and yet deny taking the bird? It doesn't make sense. Why didn't you let me know all this before, Anne? You promised to keep me informed. Remember?"

"I planned to tell you as soon as you came back. And there was nothing you could do while you were in Washington. Anyhow, it wasn't fair to trouble you with my problems when you had plenty of bigger problems to solve every day there."

"Trouble me? Sometimes I wonder if we are tuned in on the same wave length. I'll have to do something about that. In fact—"

Anne broke in hastily. "I've got a lot more to tell you. Mr. Marston called me day before yesterday. He said something serious had happened. And he was right. You remember telling me he was known as the photographic eye? Well—" She plunged into her story.

This time there was a long pause when she had finished. At last Griff said thoughtfully, "So Ned Crane tried to get some Communists up here by telling Cosgrove they wanted to buy the property you have for sale. Ned Crane! I thought he was about as low as a man could be, but this is a new low. Even for him. I'd like to know how he got to Forest Edge this afternoon. Certainly Rissa didn't invite him. That's one house he'll never enter again."

There was a long pause and then Anne said in an uncertain, tentative voice, "Griff?"

He laughed. "You said that as hesitantly as though you were afraid I'd bite."

"Not bite—but I might make you angry."

"You!" he exclaimed.

"Well, people don't like advice."

"Yours will be treasured," he said quietly.

"It's about Sharon."

"Rissa says she's been appallingly rude to you. I'll have a talk with that young lady."

"No, Griff! That's what I want to explain." Anne was silent for so long that he turned and put his hand on her shoulder, sending a tingle along her veins.

"Still afraid I'll bite?" he laughed unsteadily.

"No, I just didn't know how to put it."

"Simply and honestly, as you always do. There will never be any misunderstandings between us, Anne."

"Well, I think Sharon is falling in love with Ned Crane."

As he gave an angry growl, she said eagerly, "That's just it. Don't be angry with her, Griff. She's only seventeen and he has a great deal of charm. He can be fascinating and he can be dangerous too."

"He isn't going to be dangerous to Sharon."

Anne smiled in the dark. Men never knew very much about women.

"He has prejudiced her against all of us—you and Rissa and me. She thinks we are jealous—unfair. The more you say against him the more she will defend him. If you order him away from the house—she might—"

"I see," Griff said slowly. "But how the deuce Sharon can be taken in by a man like that—how she can defend him—is beyond me!"

"Any woman will defend the man she loves," Anne said softly. "Just because she loves him, she believes he has all the qualities she wants him to have. Be gentle with her, Griff. Make her see you couldn't do an unjust thing to save your life. She ought to know you well enough."

Careful, Anne, she warned herself in a panic. You are saying too much. Watch your step! Get a cooler tone in your voice.

There was a long silence. Several times Griff seemed about to speak. Then abruptly he changed his mind and started the motor.

"Look here, Anne," he said. "Let me take you back to Forest Edge. There is plenty of room. Rissa would be overjoyed. Under my roof I'd know you are safe."

"No," Anne said after a brief struggle with herself because she wanted so much to agree, "I won't be driven out of my own house. And I'll be safe. I lock my door at night now."

"I don't like it," he said. "I wish you'd change your mind. At least, promise me one thing. Call me or send for me if anything happens."

"But why should you—"

"Mayne Williams counted on me to be your adviser. Remember? She even—" he cleared his throat.

Not so fast, he warned himself.

"She was a wise and farsighted woman." He leaned over and kissed her on the mouth. "I'll take you home now," he said briskly.

Anne made no reply.

In front of Mountain Lodge he got out to open the door for her. He tipped back her chin so he could see her eyes. For a moment she thought he was going to kiss her again. Then he stepped back.

"Good night, darling."

"Griff," she called, "what are you going to do?"

"I'm going after that parrot," he said. "Old Soc knows something and I want to find out what it is. Lock that door, Anne!"

"Wait, Griff."

He came back to where she was standing on the steps outside the ornate front door.

"Take me with you," she pleaded.

"Heaven knows I'd like to. But better not."

"You aren't afraid of danger? Looking for a bird?"

There was a note of mockery in her voice. That's the right tone, she told herself. Light, casual, as though I don't really care what he does.

"I don't like it," Griff said. "I have a hunch—"

"Please."

He smiled and relented. "I can't refuse you anything when you look like that. We'll go together."

XIX

THE HEADLIGHTS tunneled a hole through the darkness. Griff kept his eyes on the road, part of his mind automatically intent on driving, part of it putting together the information that Anne had given him, trying to make a clear picture out of contradictory bits and pieces.

Tomorrow he would call on Gaston Cosgrove and discuss with him Minna's claim that she was married to Jimmy Williams. If that business could be cleared up once and for all the Dodges would stop their persecution of Anne. There seemed to be a clash between Dodge and Pedro Brocchi. Then why did Dodge refuse to identify Pedro? It was unlike either of the Dodges to let anyone get away with ten thousand dollars when they wanted it for their own daughter. In any case, if the Dodges attempted to make any more trouble they must go. Apparently, they had a wild idea they could bluff Anne out of the Williams fortune.

Griff came to a full stop in his thinking. He remembered Zoe Mason saying he'd have to choose between marriage and his career. If he went to Cosgrove, his political enemy, to fight for Anne's fortune, everyone would think he wanted it for himself. In that case, what was he to do?

"I've been thinking about Minna." Anne's voice came out of the darkness. "You know, Griff, I can't help feeling sorry for her."

"Forget her," Griff advised.

"With that father and mother she's never really had a chance." Anne hesitated. "Anyhow, Mrs. Williams honestly wanted her to have that money or she wouldn't have withdrawn it from the bank. I am going to ask Mr. Cosgrove to send her a check for ten thousand dollars."

As the car turned a sharp corner she swayed against him for a moment. Griff resisted the temptation to stop the car and take her in his arms. Not now, he thought. If I hurry things I may lose her. *May lose her,* indeed! How do I know that I have a chance? And it isn't fair to take advantage of a time when she's worried and frightened. What she needs right now is a friend. Period.

He sharpened to attention as he heard a creak in the back seat. Just the wind, of course. All this talk of voices in the night, strange men climbing the walls, footsteps on the path through the woods, must be getting on his nerves.

"One thing," Anne said, "if Minna *is* Mrs. Jimmy Williams I'd like to share the estate with her."

"That's ridiculous."

"Jimmy Williams died for his country," Anne said softly. "Do you think it's fair—honestly, Griff—that I should have so much and his widow so little?"

"Just suppose," Griff said, "this whole thing is a fraud? Her old friend Pedro is a self-confessed blackmailer and a thief but she doesn't attempt to give him away. Why? Because she's afraid of what will come out. I'm inclined to think Minna Dodge is heading straight for arrest."

"Oh no, Griff!"

"Don't sound so hurt and frightened, Anne. Not if you expect me to keep my mind on my driving. You may be sure nothing like that can happen without some pretty good reason."

"I suppose you're right. But to see something awful happen to her—"

"Forget it. Are you warm enough? The nights are getting cold. There's winter in the air tonight."

"I'm warm enough."

"I still think I shouldn't have let you come," Griff said uneasily.

108

Anne laughed. "You couldn't have stopped me. Griff, what will you do if you find the parrot?"

She was surprised when he took one hand from the wheel, put his arm around her and drew her close to him. With his lips to her ear he said in a low whisper, "When I say your name, duck! Understand? Hit the floor."

For an instant his warm cheek was pressed to hers and then he released her and said aloud, "Anne, let's go on to town. There's a new club where we can dance for a while."

Behind them a voice said, "You aren't going anywhere!" As Griff's foot touched the brake, the man in the back of the car said, "Keep going. I've got you covered."

Griff took a quick look at Anne by the dashboard lights. Her face was without color and her eyes were too big. But she met his gaze and she managed an uncertain smile.

He drove on. What a fool he had been to let her come with him. If anything happened to her it would be his own fault. Obviously the man must have climbed into the car unseen while he and Anne talked on the steps of Mountain Lodge.

There was no one on the road. At this time of night there was little traffic. The tourist season was over except for the skiing parties that would come later on. The highway police? Not much chance. They chiefly patrolled the roads that had heavier traffic.

The back of his neck prickled but he didn't turn his head. The unknown man, as though reading his mind, pressed cold metal against the back of his neck.

"It's loaded, buddy," he said quietly.

There must be some way of getting help. Griff went over the possibilities. Before he could turn around he would get a bullet through his head. What would happen to Anne, then?

How many dwellings would he pass? A few farms where people would be sleeping. Some deserted summer houses.

There must be some way to handle this, he thought. There has to be. I'm not going to be driven like a sheep.

As Anne shifted her position the voice warned, "Don't turn around, Miss. I won't hurt you unless I have to, but I'm not going to give you a chance to identify me."

"But I can identify you," Anne said.

Griff groaned to himself. "Quiet, Anne. You don't know what you're saying."

"Yes, I do! He's the man who broke into my house and talked to Minna, the one who chased me through the woods. He's Pedro Brocchi."

"Shut up," the man in the back of the car snarled.

"What do you intend to do?" Griff asked. "What do you want of us?"

109

Several times Pedro started to speak and each time he fell silent. He's not sure, Griff thought, with a lift of the heart, a stirring of hope. He started off half-cocked and he hasn't got a plan. I may be able to bluff him out of this yet.

"Look," Pedro said at last, "I had a different idea when I got into this car. But I kinda changed my mind. I heard what you two were saying. You've got everything figured out wrong. I could tell you some things that would surprise you."

"You can tell them to me," Griff said, "but first let me take Miss Kendrick home."

"And have her telephone the police? Nuts to that!"

Griff drove on, thinking furiously. Pedro didn't sound like the kind of man who would make up his mind in a hurry. If he could be taken by surprise—

In the distance Griff saw the lights of an approaching car. He calculated distance carefully. Fortunately, the other car was coming at a moderate speed. As it drew nearer, Griff threw his own car into a skid, shooting in front of the other and stalling the motor.

"Duck, Anne!" he yelled at the the same moment and Anne dropped to the floor of the car.

The other driver had stopped with a screaming of brakes. He opened the door.

"What are you trying to do?" he shouted.

But Griff made no answer. His door too was open and he was tearing along the road after the shadowy running figure which dodged out of the glare of the headlights.

Anne sat breathless, listening to the pounding feet. Then a surprised voice said, "Miss Kendrick! What on earth is going on here?"

"Parson Savage! I never was so glad to see anyone in my life. There was a man with a gun hiding in the back of the car. He got away when Mr. Trent managed to stop the car."

"Stop it!" The parson mopped his forehead with a handkerchief held in a shaking hand. "I thought he must be a madman. Oh, there they come."

He and Anne waited tensely while the two men came back, walking this time. Pedro came blinking into the glare of the headlights, his coat ripped and his face swollen. Behind him walked Griff, the revolver gleaming in his hand.

"Anne," he said briskly, "you drive, will you? Brocchi and I will ride in back. Oh, so it was you, Parson! I hope I didn't harm your car."

"My car's all right. But you scared me out of a year's growth. Well, Pedro! I'm sorry to see you like this. Where are you taking him, Mr. Trent?"

110

"To the police— Hey, stay where you are!" Griff ordered.

"Let me talk to you first," Pedro implored him. "Let me talk to you first. I told you that you had everything figured out wrong. Please give me a chance to explain."

As Griff hesitated the parson said, "I've known Pedro ever since he was a small boy. Won't you give him a chance to explain before turning him over to the police?"

"It won't do him any good," Griff warned.

"Please," Anne said, her voice unsteady from the strain she had been under.

Griff surrendered. "All right."

"Suppose we all go to the parsonage. I was on my way home from talking to a sick parishioner."

Parson Savage waited until Anne had backed Griff's big car and then he led the way. Anne turned the car competently and followed the red lights of the other. The two men on the back seat were silent, though Anne could see Griff's watchful face in the mirror, grimmer than she had known it could be, and intent on the prisoner beside him.

The parsonage was dark when the cars drew up before it.

"My wife has gone away for a few days to visit her mother but I'm pretty sure she left some food in the icebox," the parson said. "She always does. Miss Kendrick, let's leave these two men to have their talk while you and I forage for some food. There will be some for you too, Pedro."

"Thank you, Parson," he said in a choked voice.

In the light of the parson's old-fashioned parlor with its horsehair sofa, its old melodeon, its china lampshades, Anne got her first clear look at Pedro Brocchi. He was slim and dark, with burning eyes that seemed almost black, set in a thin, intelligent face. She recognized him as the young man who had come into the drugstore the day Tim Marston had sent for her.

Pedro did not meet her eyes or Griff's nor did he seem to be afraid of the revolver which Griff still held.

"Be careful of that," the parson said. "I think you had better give it to me, Mr. Trent. In my house, loaded weapons have never been necessary."

"It isn't loaded," Pedro admitted.

The parson looked from one man to the other and apparently he was satisfied with what he saw. He nodded his head.

"When you have finished your talk there will be a little supper in the kitchen. What my grandmother used to call a 'light collation.' Will you help me, Miss Kendrick?"

In the old-fashioned kitchen, the parson, to Anne's surprise, asked no questions. He gave her a large apron of his wife's, so big that she could almost tie it twice around her slender waist, and he began vigorously to work the pump handle at the kitchen sink.

"I'm afraid you'll spoil that lovely dress," he said in a tone of concern.

"The dress doesn't matter at all," Anne said gaily as she foraged in the icebox and took out bacon and eggs and butter.

The water came up with a gush and the parson filled the teakettle. While Anne cooked the bacon and sliced bread for toast the parson talked about Rissa's party.

"It was the most elaborate social affair we've ever had up here," he said. "History-making. My wife will never forgive herself for missing it. The Trents are one of our finest families. This community owes a lot to them. Especially to Griffith Trent. I wish we had more men like him in Congress, but I'm grateful for the ones we have."

Anne listened to him with only part of her mind, most of her attention straining for sounds from the parlor. At first there had been a sharp exchange of words. Now there was a long, steady monologue, which seemed to last forever.

Actually, it was about thirty minutes before the door opened and the two men came into the kitchen. She looked at each face but there was nothing to be read in them.

The parson took over, gave them chairs, and helped Anne serve the supper. He opened a cakebox and triumphantly took out a chocolate cake which he set down on the table.

"My wife never forgets that I like chocolate cake," he chuckled. "Whenever she goes away she leaves one for me."

Pedro and Anne were both silent but Griff talked to the parson, keeping the conversational ball rolling along on harmless subjects. Anne didn't talk because she didn't understand what was happening. Pedro sat staring at his plate.

At last Griff pushed back his chair.

"I'm afraid we'll have to be going," he said. "Thank you for your hospitality, Parson."

"I hope it was of some use to you," Parson Savage said anxiously, looking from one man to the other, his Phi Beta Kappa key swinging like a pendulum between tense fingers.

"It was. More than I can explain now." Griff looked at Pedro, who got up obediently. Whatever had happened during that long talk, all the fight seemed to have gone out of him.

"Ready, Anne?"

When they reached the car he waved Pedro to the back seat and took the wheel himself with Anne beside him.

"Where are we going?" she asked as the car moved swiftly through the night.

Griff laughed. "Where we were going in the first place when Pedro so rudely interrupted us. We are going to get Old Soc."

"Then he *did* steal the parrot," Anne whispered.

"No," Griff said in an odd tone, "it was given to him."

"*Given!* But who—"

"The generous donor was Ned Crane."

"Griff, that's impossible! Ned Crane wasn't even here. He was in New York when that parrot was stolen from Mrs. Williams. He simply couldn't—"

"When it was stolen the first time, yes. But it seems that the night I threw Crane over the wall he didn't go back to the Inn, after all. He hung around the club."

"The man in the tree!" Anne said in excitement.

"Yes, Crane was the man in the tree who overheard what Joe told you about finding the parrot. He tracked it down that night, stole it from the farmer, leaving Joe's muffler as a kind of red herring, and took it to Pedro."

"But why?"

"I'll tell you about that later. Meanwhile, Anne—" his voice was deadly serious—"you are not to breathe a word of this to anyone. *Anyone,* you understand?"

"Yes, Simon Legree," she said, trying to speak lightly, though her heart was thumping.

The village was dark. Only a few lights burned here and there.

Griff stopped the car in front of the garage. "I'll be back in a minute, Anne," he said. "Wait here for me." He changed his mind. "No, I don't like to leave you alone. You had better come along." He helped her out of the car and his hand kept a tight hold on hers. "I can see that I'm not going to have any peace of mind unless I stick to you in the future like a Seeing-Eye dog." His voice dropped to a whisper. "Would you mind very much?"

"Be careful," Pedro said. Anne started, because it was the first time he had spoken since they had begun the drive. "It's dark out here."

He led the way to a door at the back of the garage. Anne heard a key rattle in the lock.

"That's queer," he muttered. "I must have forgotten to lock the door. Or else—"

Griff's hand tightened on Anne's. Pedro turned a switch and a single drop light revealed steep, narrow stairs leading to the apartment over the garage. He led the way.

At the top he opened a door onto a small, bare-looking room holding a cot, a table, a couple of rickety chairs and a chest of drawers. On the table stood a big covered bird cage.

Pedro pulled back the cover and clucked.

There was no answering sound from the bunch of gray feathers lying on the bottom of the cage.

Griff exclaimed and leaned closer to the cage.

"Careful," Pedro warned him. "If he doesn't like you he's liable to take a peck with that beak of his."

"No," Griff told him. "He'll never do that again."

"Why?"

"Because someone beat us to it," Griff said. "The bird is dead."

XX

"I'VE ALWAYS liked this room," Tim Marston said. "The kind of room a man dreams of, where he can read and work and think and dream undisturbed."

Griff's study at Forest Edge was lined with books, whose gleaming leather bindings reflected the light from a great log blazing in the huge fireplace. Deep, comfortable, maroon leather chairs, a workmanlike desk and big table, and lights which enabled one to read in comfort without glare, explained the druggist's enthusiasm.

Heavy green drapes that matched the carpet had been drawn across the windows, shutting out the gray twilight. With bowls of massed autumn flowers on table, desk and mantel, the room was warm and bright.

Over the mantel hung a portrait of Rissa as she had been five years ago, her dark-brown hair in a soft pompadour, bare shoulders and arms gleaming in a white evening dress.

"I like this room, too," Griff said. He looked up at the portrait with an affectionate smile. "Rissa planned it for me. Whatever charm Forest Edge may have is owing to her. That sister of mine is a born homemaker."

"And a superb hostess," said the third man in the group sitting in front of the crackling fire.

Griff, who was lighting his pipe, stole a quick look at John Clinton's face. Apparently, his matchmaking ideas were not so bad. Clinton seemed barely able to take his eyes off Rissa's face when they were together and, unless I mistake the signs, Griff thought, she feels the same way. There is a softer quality about her these last few days. A kind of glow. And a dreamy look in her eyes.

I hope it works out. John Clinton should go far. There is a look of greatness about him. And he is a stanch friend. I'd like to have him for a brother-in-law.

For a few minutes the three men sat smoking quietly, looking into the fire. Then Clinton said, "What is it all about, Griff? What are we three supposed to be in conference about?"

"It seems," Griff told him, "that while you and I have been trying to look after our country's best interests in Washington, something has been going on under our very noses. An attempt has been made at Communist infiltration up here."

Clinton sat up with a jerk.

Griff turned to Marston. "Miss Kendrick told me about her conversation with you. I'd like to get the whole story."

Marston nodded. "As I explained to Miss Kendrick, it all goes back to what people call my photographic eye. When I see a person once I never forget the face. It's permanently registered in my memory."

"That's a useful gift," Clinton commented. "I'd like to have that myself. Meeting so many people at political affairs, I find it difficult to remember them all and they are invariably hurt when I don't."

"I've had the same experience," Griff said feelingly.

"Anyhow," Marston went on, "the FBI thought it might be useful to them. So they arranged to smuggle me into some Communist meetings they got wind of. All I was supposed to do was to memorize those faces and sing out if I ever saw any of them again."

He tossed his cigarette into the fire. "Imagine my surprise and consternation when I saw three of them right here in town. I asked around and found out they had all come up to buy the property Miss Kendrick had for sale. And they seemed to have a lot of friends who were after the same thing."

The druggist took off his glasses and polished them absently while he talked.

"I asked Miss Kendrick to come to see me, told her about it, and she didn't waste a minute." He chuckled. "Next time anyone talks to me about brainless beauty I am going to point to her to prove the old phrase isn't so. She telephoned Mr. Cosgrove and stopped the sale then and there. Cosgrove put up an argument, said it was too late in the day to do anything, but Miss Kendrick made clear that either he would handle her affairs her way or else. So he stopped the sale."

"Cosgrove," John Clinton said thoughtfully. "That name rings a bell. Oh, of course, he's your political antagonist this fall, isn't he, Griff?"

"Cosgrove is in the clear on this," Marston said quickly. "I can't say I like him very much. I certainly hope he won't get Griff's seat in Congress. But he was taken in. After all, no one would run around checking on a person's political affiliations when he buys a piece of property. And Cosgrove wouldn't take a fool chance like that. He wouldn't jeopardize his political career. One word about a Communist tie-in would finish him."

"Then what brought these people up here?" Clinton asked.

Griff was silent, listening, making no contribution.

"Not *what*," Marston corrected. "*Who*. A man named Ned Crane."

Again Griff made no comment, showed no surprise. It was almost, Clinton thought, as though he had known all this before.

"Crane!" Clinton exclaimed. "For the love of Mike! He's that good-looking fellow who was paying so much attention to little Sharon at your party. Why the—"

"Steady there." Griff spoke at last. "Take it easy, fella. You needn't worry about Ned Crane. Time is running out for him."

"What do you mean?"

"The FBI is closing in. They are on their way up here now to pick him up."

Marston nodded. "They certainly work fast. They arrested his friends when they got off the train at Grand Central Station in New York after Cosgrove refused to go through with the sale."

"I hope they give Crane the works," Clinton said heatedly. "So long as I live I'll never understand why men betray their country. What makes them do it?"

"In this case," Marston said, "it's just plain hard cash. I'm not at liberty to pass on all I've heard even to you gentlemen, but I can give you the general picture. The FBI men checked on Crane. He is nothing but a slick confidence man. Comes from a good family, had a fine education, but he was an only child and his mother pampered him. He thought there must be an easier way to get rich than working for it. He wanted to marry money. He has been married twice to rich women—"

This time Griff was really surprised. He gave a startled exclamation.

"He ran through their money and they divorced him. I understand he nearly brought off a third rich marriage a couple of years ago but something broke it up. It's easy for anyone who knew his history to figure he would be for sale to the highest bidder. I don't know just how the Communists got hold of him, but he must have profited by it—or expected to profit by it. His mind works that way."

Clinton edged his chair a little closer to the fire. Griff noticed it.

"Chilly in here," he said. "There must be a draft somewhere."

He got up as Marston rose to his feet.

"I must get back to the drugstore. Sometimes I think a solitary druggist in a community is as hard-ridden as an old-fashioned country practitioner. Never dares be out of reach for fear an emergency will come up."

The druggist shook hands with the two men, and Griff went to the door with him. On his way back to the fireplace he noticed that one of the drapes was stirring gently. He pulled it back.

"No wonder you were cold, John! One of the windows is wide open. I wonder the maid didn't notice it when she drew the drapes."

He closed the window and came back to his chair. Clinton sat without moving, his eyes on Rissa's portrait. When he saw that Griff was watching him he smiled broadly.

"Griff," he said, "I want your congratulations."

"Really? Why?"

"This afternoon I asked your sister to marry me and she said she would."

Griff jumped to his feet and the two men shook hands warmly.

"I congratulate you both. There isn't a man I'd rather see Rissa marry."

"Thanks, Griff. I believe you mean that. I don't deserve her."

"She's a wonderful person," Griff said. "And she's had a lot of unhappiness. I can't tell you how glad I am to have it come to an end at last. To have a wholly new life start for her."

"I'll do all a man can to make her happy," Clinton promised. As he looked at Griff his eyes narrowed. "What's wrong? Why are you worrying? Do you doubt that I will be able to make her happy?"

"Great Scott, no! But I was just wondering—does Rissa fully realize that your work keeps you in Washington?"

"That's one of the wonderful things about it," Clinton exclaimed. "She's making all sorts of plans. She not only wants to be my hostess, to help me with all the social burdens of my position; she even wants to be my secretary."

"Then everything is perfect!" Griff's face lighted up in a relieved smile. At last Rissa was truly free of Ned Crane. She could return to the city where he had hurt her so badly, turn over a new leaf and look forward to the future with the past forgotten.

Leaving his future brother-in-law dreaming beside the

fire, Griff went in search of his sister. He found her just returning from a long walk, a navy-blue cape over her shoulders, her cheeks flushed and eyes bright from the exercise.

"Griff," she began eagerly, the color deepening in her cheeks, "has John told you?"

"Just now." He kissed her warmly. "You are going to be a happy woman, Rissa, as happy as you have always deserved to be. And thank you for giving me such a nice brother-in-law." He grinned at her. "I couldn't have chosen better for you myself."

She laughed. "It's strange, Griff, how hard it is to get used to the idea of being happy."

"You'll get used to it."

"If only you could have the same happiness." She hesitated. "Since Zoe jilted you, there have been times when I thought you would never love another woman. But lately—"

He interrupted her hastily. "John tells me you're going to live in Washington."

She lifted her head proudly. "Why not? There's no more interesting city in the world today. And there are so many things I can do to help John. My head is simply bursting with plans."

He shook his head at her, smiling. "The same old Rissa! It looks to me as though I'll have to find someone else to look after me. You've been more help than I can say."

Her eyes were shadowed. "Griff—"

"Hey," he laughed. "You mustn't take me seriously. Things have turned out exactly the way I hoped they would."

Rissa glanced at her watch. "Heavens, I didn't know it was so late. I walked longer than I intended and lost track of time. I'll have to hurry and dress for dinner. Where is Sharon?"

"I haven't seen her all afternoon."

"That's odd. Oh, well, she's probably in her room."

Rissa went swiftly up the stairs, tall and graceful, the cape floating around her, a new spring in her step.

Half an hour later she came down, dressed for dinner, looking radiantly lovely. At first Griff was aware that there was something different about her. Then he realized that she had discarded the lilac which she'd worn for two years. Instead, she wore a long white dress with a full skirt and a short scarlet jacket, with matching slippers.

The two men exchanged admiring glances as she came toward them. She looked around and frowned.

"Where is Sharon? Hasn't she come down yet?"

"I haven't seen her."

"Griff! You mean she hasn't come home? She wasn't in her room when I went upstairs."

"She must be in the house somewhere," Griff said. "She wouldn't have gone out with that bad cold. After her illness last year she knows what a risk it is."

"I'm worried, Griff."

He started to speak, saw her drawn face.

"We'll organize a search party," he said briskly. "You and John go through the house. I'll get the gardener and we'll go over the grounds."

Half an hour later the two searching parties converged in the hallway. Sharon wasn't in the house.

Sharon wasn't anywhere.

XXI

ANNE SAT alone at the big dining table, wearing a black crepe dinner dress with bishop sleeves and a long, full skirt. Her slim waist was encircled by a belt of gold links. Her hair, touched by the candlelight, gleamed like honey.

As she ate her broiled grapefruit she watched Dodge from under her long lashes. Even on her first night in this house she had been aware that he was attempting to establish himself in the driver's seat. Tonight there was no trace of his former impeccable service. It had been indifferent, even careless. The butler was acting very much as though he were the real master here and no longer cared what she thought about it. There was a malicious triumph in his face that disturbed her.

I'm too tired to tackle a problem like Dodge tonight, she thought. Tomorrow I'll see Mr. Cosgrove and ask him to dismiss the Dodges and give them their pension. Then I'll be free of them.

The butler had left the room. He returned now to say, "Miss Trent is on the telephone. She is sorry to disturb you at dinner but it is urgent."

Anne ran down to the telephone. There really should be some extensions in this big house, she thought.

"Hello, Rissa," she called gaily.

"Anne." The older woman's voice was high-pitched with tension. "Is Sharon with you?"

"Why no, she isn't."

"Have you seen her at all today?"

"What's happened?"

Over the wire she heard a choked cry. "She isn't there, Griff," and the sound of heartbroken sobbing.

Then Griff said quietly, "Sharon seems to have disappeared, Anne. We've looked everywhere. Rissa hoped perhaps she was with you."

"But where could she have gone?"

"I'm afraid I have an idea of what happened," Griff said. "Someone overheard a conversation this afternoon in which I said the FBI was on the way to pick up Crane. I think that someone was Sharon. I'm afraid she's gone to warn him."

"What are you going to do?"

"I'm on my way to the Inn now to find out whether that crazy niece of mine has gone there to see Crane."

"Let me know, won't you?"

"Of course. Don't worry too much, dear. I'm sure she'll be all right."

For a few minutes Anne stood beside the silent telephone. Those tender words of Griff's had probably been addressed to Rissa, not to her. She thought furiously. Griff was right, of course. Sharon was infatuated; she believed everyone was against Crane and unfair to him. It would be like her warmhearted loyalty to warn him, protect him.

But what would Crane do? He must realize by now that his plans had all failed. Anne could not marry him. He had been detected in his Communist deal. He would try to salvage what he could—marry Sharon and her third of the Trent money.

Anne went up to the game room and paced slowly up and down. *What would Crane do?* As soon as he knew his danger he would leave the Inn at once. He had a head start. Griff would never find him there. He would try to conceal Sharon until he could talk her into an elopement. But where? Where?

The apartment over the garage! Pedro Brocchi had told Griff he was going to leave it, move to the Inn and stay there openly. No more hole-and-corner stuff. What *had* Pedro and Griff talked about? No time for that now.

Crane knew about the apartment. He had brought the parrot there. It was a good place to hide. Anne ran down the stairs to the telephone and then stopped short. Griff would already have left the house.

She called the Inn. "Mr. Trent is on his way there," she said breathlessly. "Will you please take a message? This is Miss Kendrick calling. Please tell him I said—" she thought for a moment— "I said to look where he found the parrot."

"Excuse me, Miss," said a dazed voice. "It sounded as though you said parrot."

"I did say parrot."

"Yes, Miss."

"You'll be sure Mr. Trent gets that message?"

"Yes, Miss."

Anne turned away from the telephone. "I'm going out, Dodge. Will you get my car out at once."

"Yes, Miss Kendrick."

Anne looked unseeingly at the wall. Then she ran up the stairs, pulled on a black cape lined with green, with a hood faced in the same color. She raced down the stairs. The car was in front of the door.

"If anyone calls I'll be back within an hour." I hope, she added silently to herself.

She let in the clutch and was off. My hunch may be all wrong, she thought, but I've got to be sure. I don't dare wait. Suppose Ned persuades Sharon to elope with him? I've got to get there first.

She took a curve too fast. Watch it, Anne. If you have an accident now you may hurt more than yourself. Sharon is so trusting, so young, only seventeen.

Only seventeen, she thought more clearly. Of course, why didn't I remember that before? Her heart pounded with excitement. *I know I'm right.*

Her teeth were chattering. She turned on the heater, rolled up the window, pulled the hood down over her head. Last time she had driven over this road, Pedro had said from the back seat, "You aren't going anywhere. I've got you covered."

She wanted to turn her head, to look behind her, but she dared not stop. There wasn't a moment to lose. Last time Griff had been beside her, his cheek pressed against hers. She hadn't been afraid, because he was there.

Br-r-r! It was getting colder every minute. A wind swept down from the mountain and seemed to pull at the car with a giant hand. It was hard to keep it on the road.

Past the intersection that led onto the main highway. Past a summer house, windows boarded up for the winter. Past a farmhouse, sleeping through the night. Past a dirt road that led to the parsonage. Past a car stalled on the road, a man changing a flat tire by flarelight. Bad luck. In the rear-view mirror she saw him run out into the road, waving madly at her. Sorry, she thought. I hate to leave a fellow driver in trouble. But I can't waste any time on you tonight.

Slower now for the village. A dim light in the butcher shop. Lights shining from the Inn a mile beyond the village.

How far that little candle throws his beams!
So shines a good deed in a naughty world.

The familiar lines came into Anne's mind and were forgotten again as she drove up to the dark garage. No, better

121

not park where Crane would be sure to see and recognize her car. She drove on a little distance, locked the car and pulled the cape closely around her as she felt the icy fingers of the wind.

As she walked back to the garage her high heels tapped sharply on the pavement, sounding as loud as hammers in the quiet night. She tried to muffle her footsteps, to walk softly.

There was no sound as she reached the garage. It seemed to be dark and deserted. She went around to the back. No light in the windows. Suppose she was wrong! Suppose Sharon was somewhere else?

No, she must be here, Anne thought. Ned wouldn't dare be seen talking to her at the Inn. He'll know that's the first place Griff will look for her. He'll have to take her somewhere to talk. There's no other place. They *have* to be here.

She tilted back her head, looking up.

Wasn't there a thin pencil of light at the edge of the drawn shades? Glory be, someone was in the apartment! A stone rolled and her heart leaped in her throat. She wheeled around. Nothing but a shadow in the moonlight cast by a big elm tree.

She went to the door, walking on tiptoe, took hold of the knob and turned it. The door was unlocked. For a moment she looked up the narrow, dark staircase. She didn't dare turn on the light. Her breath was coming unsteadily.

I don't like the dark. I don't want to go up there. Suppose it isn't Sharon? Suppose someone else is there?

She hesitated, afraid to go in. She looked back and then pressed her hand over her mouth to hold back a scream. The shadow of the elm tree had moved. Now there were two shadows!

For a moment she stood paralyzed. Then she opened the door and slipped inside. She closed it and leaned against it until she could get her breath.

What am I going to do? I'm afraid to go back. I'm afraid to go ahead.

In a moment her heart had steadied. Anne Kendrick, she scolded herself, are you afraid of shadows? I'm ashamed of you. Stop thinking about yourself and think about Sharon.

Slowly, one hand against the wall, she groped her way up the stairs. The darkness seemed to enclose her, to shut her in. At the top of the stairs her heel came down hard as she miscalculated and reached for another step. The noise sounded deafening.

She waited a moment. Looked down at the door at the foot of the steps. Looked at the thin golden light showing under the apartment door. She moved forward on tiptoe, holding her breath, listening.

There were voices now, too low-pitched to carry. She put her head against the door. Then she heard Sharon saying, "Of course I believe you, Ned! I've never doubted you for a moment."

"Then you'll marry me?"

There was a little pause and then the girl spoke, sounding very young, very uncertain. "Ned, are you sure you love me?"

He laughed confidently. Anne strained but she could not make out the words he was murmuring.

"Marry you—right away?" Sharon gasped. Ned murmured again.

"All right," she said at last. "But I wish I could tell Aunt Rissa first. She has been so kind to me, even if she is unjust to you."

Below Anne there was a faint creak but she heard it only subconsciously. All her attention was fixed on the voices from behind the door. Her fingers moved over it lightly, seeking for the knob. She turned it and went in.

Sharon, in a gray wool dress with a red leather belt, a red scarf knotted around her neck and a red corduroy coat that made a warm spot of color in the drab room, was sitting on one of the rickety chairs at the table, on which still stood the empty parrot cage. Her cheeks were flushed and her eyes misty with unshed tears.

Ned Crane, dapper as usual in a perfectly fitting dinner jacket, stood with his back to the door, looking down at her.

It was Sharon who saw Anne first. Her eyes grew round with surprise and consternation.

"How did you find me?" she gasped.

Crane turned swiftly. When he saw Anne his smiling mouth hardened into grimness.

"Sharon," Anne said, coming forward into the room, "I want to talk to you."

"Don't listen to her, my sweet," Crane said to Sharon. "She'll only try to poison your mind against me."

"Your Aunt Rissa is nearly crazy with worry," Anne began.

For a moment the girl's expression of defiance wavered.

"Please let me take you home, Sharon," Anne pleaded.

"No," Sharon said. "No. I'm going to marry Ned Crane tonight. No one can stop me."

Then Anne turned to Crane. The hood fell back on her neck, revealing the bright hair. She met his eyes steadily. He gave her a sardonic smile, not attempting to conceal his triumph.

"You heard her," he jeered. "She is going to marry me tonight and there is nothing you can do about it."

"You are wrong." Anne spoke slowly and distinctly.

123

"There's a lot that can be done about it. You can't marry Sharon."

"Why not?"

"Because," Anne told him, "she's under age. She is only seventeen."

There was a pause while Crane absorbed the shock. His eyes stared blankly. His mouth hung open.

"Is that true?" he asked Sharon hoarsely.

She nodded her head, ashamed at being caught in her childish deception.

"But why," he began to shout furiously, "didn't you tell me the truth in the first place? Why did you pretend you were nineteen?"

"Ned," she wailed, her face white as his angry words struck her like so many blows.

Anne started to protest and stopped herself. No, she thought, it is better for her to be hurt now. She will see what he is really like. The cure will be the more complete.

"Why did you lie to me?" Ned shouted.

"I just thought," Sharon sobbed, "if you believed I was older you wouldn't—" the sobs grew heavier—"t-t-treat me like s-s-such a kid."

"You see," Anne's voice rang out defiantly, "it's no use. If you elope with Sharon the marriage won't be legal. You'll never be able to lay your hands on Sharon's money."

"Money," Sharon scoffed. "As though that mattered to Ned."

"Doesn't it, Sharon?" Anne said softly. "Look at his face."

Sharon looked up. The handsome face was changed beyond recognition, the nostrils distended, the lips drawn back from his teeth in rage. He was out of control.

"You little fool! When I think of the risk I've taken, wasting valuable time with you when I could be getting away—" he yelled at Sharon.

"Don't you love me any more?" she asked, as though she still could not believe it.

"Love you! If you'd told me the truth in the beginning, do you think I'd have wasted two minutes on you?"

He jerked at his topcoat and flung himself into it. He grabbed up his hat, pushed Anne to one side, and they heard his feet clatter down the stairs.

Sharon dropped her head on her arms, crying aloud like a desolate small child. Anne moved toward her, one hand outstretched in sympathy. Better not, she decided, and the hand dropped to her side. She doesn't want my sympathy. Not yet, anyhow. I'd better sit down before my knees give way.

She sank into the other chair. Crane's footsteps had

stopped abruptly. Was he coming back? She tensed. Then she heard him say savagely, "What are you doing here?"

"Looking for you. Just in time, I see." It was Pedro Brocchi's voice.

Sharon's sobs broke off, catching in her throat as she heard the men's voices. She too was listening.

"Out of my way," Crane said. "I'm in a hurry."

"I'll bet you are." Pedro laughed. "You've never said a truer word."

Then there was the sound of a brief scuffle. Pedro said mockingly, "Not so fast, Crane. Not so fast."

"Let me past!"

"No."

There was a blow, another, then the frail railing shook as the men battered at each other in the dark on the narrow staircase. Their heavy panting breath, grunts as they were hit, a muffled oath.

Sharon lifted her tear-stained face. One hand groped for Anne, who held it in her own. Sharon clung to it feverishly, like a lost child.

There was a crash that brought the girls to their feet, a sound of falling, a metallic click. Silence.

Were they both dead? What had happened out there in the dark?

Footsteps again. One pair. Coming up the stairs. Pedro Brocchi stood in the doorway, his coat ripped, his collar hanging open, his nose bleeding. He stanched it with a handkerchief.

For a moment he looked from one to the other, panting. Then he said, "You girls had better go home. There is nothing you can do here and you don't want to get involved in this."

"What happened to him?" Anne asked.

Pedro grinned, and his face looked more boyish than Anne had ever seen it. Then it sobered. "I knocked him out. He's handcuffed. You had better get away before—" he stopped hastily as though afraid he had said too much.

Anne led Sharon out of the room. The light was on and the stairs were empty. At the bottom Ned Crane lay in a heap, his hands handcuffed behind him, his eyes closed. Slowly the two girls edged down the stairs, past him.

Crane's eyes fluttered open, he stirred uneasily, saw the two girls.

"Sharon," he said pleadingly.

For a long moment she looked down at him. Then she turned away.

"Ready, Anne?" she asked, stepped around him, and went out the door.

XXII

"I'LL BRING her back, Rissa. Don't worry," Griff called to his sister as he ran out to the big, low-hung car which, according to Anne, could do a million miles an hour.

With a low throb the car sped down the highway. I'm taking it too fast, he thought, racing along the road, but for once in my life I've got to take a chance.

How long has Sharon been gone? She must have been out walking, heard my conference with John Clinton and Marston, caught Crane's name and listened. She has an hour's start at most.

But how did she get down to the Inn—if she has gone to the Inn. I'm guessing at that. She didn't drive. She must have taken her bicycle. Wish I'd thought to look.

This is the third time Crane has crossed my path. First he tried to marry Rissa and her money. His own greed betrayed him then. And now, thank God, Rissa has another chance at happiness. Then he tried to capture Anne and the Williams fortune. Her own sound instinct prevented that. And this time he is after Sharon and her money.

There was an explosion and the car swerved. It required all Griff's strength to hold it on the road. For a split second he thought he had been shot at. Then he realized it was a blowout. He drew off on the side of the road and leaped out of the car, started a flare to warn other cars and give him some light to work by, ripped off his coat and got to work.

Fortunately, there was a spare tire in the luggage compartment. He worked like mad. Took off the tire, rolled it to one side, lifted on the new one.

Lights. A car coming. It passed, going fast. Anne's car. Anne at the wheel.

Griff tore out into the road, waving frantically. "Anne!" he shouted. "Anne! Stop!" But she was driving too fast. She was out of hearing range.

He went back, working at top speed. I'll bet this is the world's record for changing a tire, he thought. He realized that the landscape was flooded with milky light. The moon was full.

He put the old tire in the luggage compartment, ran around and started the car. In a moment he was driving at headlong speed along the road which Anne had just taken, trying to make up for lost time. But where was she going? And at such a speed. It wasn't safe for her. Nothing must happen to Anne.

Queer he hadn't overtaken her by now. Unless she has turned off somewhere. But where could she be going?

The lights of the Inn were ahead, music coming from the dining room. He parked the car and hurried inside. No sign of Sharon and Crane in the lobby. He followed the sound of music. Only a few couples were dining. The two people he sought were not at the tables, not among the dancers in the cleared space in the center.

"Table for you, Mr. Trent?" the headwaiter asked, hastening up to greet him.

"No thanks, just looking for someone."

I can't let it be public knowledge that Sharon is missing, he thought. I can't ask for her.

"Is Mr. Crane here?"

"No, sir. I haven't seen him tonight. Usually he dines here regularly. You might try the cocktail lounge."

Griff nodded, went back to the lobby and down a couple of steps into the dimly lighted cocktail lounge. It was empty except for a bartender.

He called to a passing bellhop: "Where is Mr. Crane's room?"

"Number twenty-two on the second floor, sir. End of the corridor to your left."

Griff took the stairs two at a time. He was aware of a growing sense of urgency.

He knocked on the door bearing the number 22 and, getting no answer, turned the knob. The room was empty. Worse than that, the closet was empty and so were the dresser drawers. It looked as though Crane had made his getaway. With Sharon?

Griff ran down the stairs again. Went to the desk. "Have you seen Mr. Crane this evening?"

"Yes, sir. Your niece, Miss Ames, called to see him. I saw them talking in the lobby. Then they went out."

Griff tried to conceal the fact that he had been dealt a blow. Too late! Too late!

"Thank you," he said casually. "I must have missed them. We were all planning to meet but we must have got our arrangements mixed up."

He was nearly at the door before the desk clerk caught up with him.

"Mr. Trent! There's a message for you. Miss Kendrick telephoned. She said to tell you—" he looked down at the message in his hand—"it sounds silly but it's her exact words—"

"Go on," Griff said in an agony of impatience.

"She said to look where you found the parrot."

For a moment Griff's face was blank. Then his eyes blazed. "By George," he exclaimed, "I believe she's right."

He plunged out of the Inn and in a moment the long car rocketed out of the driveway, back in the direction from which it had come.

The desk clerk stared after it, shaking his head. "If you ask me," he said aloud, addressing the empty lobby, "they're both crazy."

As the car plummeted along the road back to the village, Griff thought, Anne is right. Crane has taken Sharon to Pedro's apartment to talk to her. He knew we'd catch him at the Inn. Pray God, I'm not too late.

That's where Anne must have been going. Doesn't waste a minute. Who said that? Oh, yes, Marston when he was speaking of Anne this afternoon.

I could have told him a lot about Anne Kendrick after studying her for two years. I could have told him of the courageous way she set to work to earn a living, asking nothing of her stepmother. About her talent and her hard work. About watching her programs and hearing her clear, soaring voice that wrapped itself around my heart. About seeing her earnest face in the finance class. About seeing her dance and envying her partners and wanting to dance with her myself, to hold her in my arms.

Hey, fella. Stop raving. You have work to do. Keep your mind on the job.

The car swung into the main street of the village. To Griff's surprise the drugstore was ablaze with light. In front of it was the limousine from the airport and beside it stood a group of men.

What goes on here, Griff thought, but he drove on toward the garage and Pedro's apartment.

A man ran out from the group yelling, "Hey, Trent! Trent! Stop!"

Griff put on the brake and then backed toward the drugstore. The man who had hailed him was the druggist himself.

"I can't stop now, Marston," Griff called. "I'm in a frightful rush. I'll be back later."

"No! Wait a minute. The FBI men are here." The druggist beckoned and the men came up to the car. There were three of them, young, alert, clean-cut. Griff looked them over with approval. Good men to have on your side, he thought.

The druggist introduced them. "They got here sooner than I expected. Flew up from Washington and called me from the airfield. We're on the way to the Inn to pick up Ned Crane."

"He's not there." Griff explained swiftly what had happened.

"Where is this garage?" one of the Federal men asked.

Griff pointed it out.

"All right, leave your car here. We'll walk." Swiftly the man made his plans, assigned a task to each of his companions. "Want to come along to see the fun?" he asked Griff.

"When that rat probably has my niece up there? Try to stop me!"

"Okay. Let's get going. Spread out, boys. Surround the place. And no talking. You know what to do when you get there."

They nodded grimly. They knew what to do, all right.

So when Anne and Sharon opened the door at the foot of the stairs, they walked into the arms of the FBI. Sharon caught sight of Griff standing behind the others in the spot that had been assigned to him.

"Uncle Griff!" she cried and flung herself into his arms.

He held her tenderly but over her curly head he looked at Anne.

"Are you all right, Sharon?"

"Yes, but I'm just so darned mad, Uncle Griff!"

In his relief he laughed out loud. "And you?" he asked Anne.

"Yes. Pedro Brocchi has Ned Crane tied up. Who are these men?"

"Government. Everything is under control now."

The young man in charge gave Anne a quick measuring glance in which there was considerable admiration, and then he went inside.

Griff led Sharon to Anne. For a moment his fingers rested lightly on her shoulder. "I have a lot to thank you for, Anne. You did a brave thing tonight."

"I just thought of this place and I didn't dare wait."

"I know. Will you take Sharon back to Forest Edge and wait until I come?"

There was an enraged shout from Ned Crane and a curt order. Crane fell silent.

"I may be busy here for a while," Griff said in a tone of satisfaction. "See you later."

Anne drove slowly back to Forest Edge. Sharon sat huddled beside her. She had not spoken once but, at least, she had stopped crying. Not until they turned into the driveway at Forest Edge did she break the silence.

"Anne," she said in a small voice, "I've been such an awful droop. Can you forgive me?"

Anne laughed. "I was never mad at you."

A stream of light blazed from the front porch as the door was flung open and Rissa came running out to welcome them.

"Sharon?" A quick anxious look and Rissa's face lighted. "Anne! I was never so relieved—"

"Come in, girls, or you'll freeze." John Clinton led them into the house, where Zoe Mason sat in a backless, strapless coral net dress with a bouffant skirt, her eyes bright with curiosity.

As Rissa chattered on in her relief, Clinton said, "These girls are half frozen, and I don't think Sharon has had any dinner."

"I haven't. And I'm starving." Sharon looked at her aunt, dreading the scolding she thought she deserved, but Clarissa Trent was giving orders for a tray to be served to Miss Sharon at once.

"And don't spare the food," Sharon called.

Clinton kept the conversation on safe lines until Sharon had finished cold sliced chicken, a salad and a frozen dessert. She sat back sipping a glass of milk.

"All right," she said, "scold me. I know just how idiotic I've been. I should have known you better, Aunt Rissa. I should have known you and Uncle Griff wouldn't be unfair or unjust. Only I trusted Ned—" Her voice quavered for a moment. Then she lifted her chin. "But ber-lieve me, I'm cured."

Rissa laughed. "Just for that, I have something nice for you."

"A present!" Sharon squealed, and Anne wondered how Crane had ever thought this child was grown-up.

Rissa handed her a letter.

"From Joe Bennet!" Sharon ripped open the envelope and read it quickly.

"Gee," she said at last, "I hope he never finds out what a dope I was. Being taken in by a traitor when he is in the Marines. You know what Joe says? He says, 'I hope, by the time I get back to civilian life, you'll be grown-up.'"

She leaned her head against her chair. "I wonder why he said that?" Her eyelids fell, her head slipped to one side. She was sound asleep.

John Clinton picked her up gently and, with Rissa leading the way, carried Sharon up to her room.

Anne sat looking into the fire.

"Well," Zoe said lightly. "Sharon seems to have landed herself in a mess. Communists, of all things. Poor Griff! This will really queer his chances."

A car door slammed and in a moment Griff came into the room.

"Where is everyone?"

Anne explained and he nodded.

"Really, darling, you aren't very tactful," Zoe drawled.

130

"What do you mean—where is everyone? I'm here. Or don't you think I'm anyone?"

"Hello there, Zoe." As Clinton came down the stairs Griff said, "John, I'm going to drive back to Mountain Lodge with Miss Kendrick. Will you follow in my car and pick me up there?"

"Of course."

Anne got wearily to her feet. She felt too tired from the reaction to know what she was doing. She would have walked straight into the fireplace if Griff had not caught her arm.

"Hey," he said, "you aren't going to collapse, are you?"

"No. But I feel as though I could sleep for a week."

As he led her toward the door, Zoe said sharply, "Griff, have you made up your mind about that career of yours?"

What did Zoe mean by that, Anne wondered sleepily, watching Griff's profile as he drove her car.

"I'm not going to ask you tonight to tell me what happened," he said. "You're too tired. There will be plenty of time for that later."

He stopped the car below the flight of steps that led up to the impressive entrance of Mountain Lodge. He wanted to take her in his arms. The thought of it sent the blood coursing through his veins.

Behind him Clinton had brought the other car to a stop. Griff helped Anne out and took her up to the door.

"Good night, Anne," he said with restraint. "Get a good rest."

"What happens next?" she asked him. "What are we going to do now?"

"We wait," he said.

XXIII

"WE WAIT" Griffith Trent had said. And they waited. After the excitement of the past weeks Anne found that period of inactivity almost more than she could bear.

Things were happening. She was aware of that. But no one told her anything. There was no word about Ned Crane. Cosgrove did not keep his promise to call her in a few days about the "grave developments." Pedro had dropped out of sight. There was no sign of Minna. Was she staying at Mountain Lodge or had she returned to New York? Anne found herself feeling sorry for Minna without quite knowing why. Dodge offered no information and Anne asked for none.

Worst of all, Griffith Trent didn't come to see her. He

didn't telephone. He might have forgotten her existence except for the cellophane box that arrived, holding long-stemmed red roses. Under the flowers was his card and scrawled on it were the words, *Perhaps Mayme Williams did leave you a husband.*

And that was all. When Anne couldn't stand waiting any longer, she went to see Parson Savage and asked him to put her to work. He let her take over a group of small children to entertain while their mothers did their week's shopping. Playing games with the children and singing to them released some of her tension.

Next day the silence and the waiting came to an end.

That morning Rissa telephoned to say Sharon was in bed with a bad cold but otherwise all right.

"Griff told me how brave and wonderful you were, Anne. There's no adequate way to thank you. As soon as I can leave Sharon, I'll be seeing you." Before hanging up, she asked, "Have you heard about Ned Crane?"

"I haven't heard about anything," Anne wailed. "I might as well be living at the bottom of a mine."

Rissa laughed. "The FBI took him to New York. According to the message Griff got, he is 'threatening' to talk, whatever that means."

It was shortly after that telephone conversation that Anne heard the professionally trained voice singing a Spanish song. At first she thought it was the radio. Della, the blond parlormaid who hated Dodge, was polishing the brasswork around the fireplace in the game room when the song rang out.

The maid looked at Anne and away again as though uncertain.

"What is it, Della?" Anne said in a kindly tone. "Is there something you want to tell me?"

The maid looked over her shoulder. "If Mr. Dodge finds out I told you . . ." she muttered.

"Don't be silly!" Anne said. "He can't hurt you."

"You don't know him, Miss." The maid sidled closer to Anne, her voice almost a whisper. "I'll take a chance. The whole staff thinks you ought to know what's going on here."

Anne smiled encouragement but her heart swelled with indignation. Dodge has got to go, she thought. I won't permit him to terrorize these people the way he does. I have no right to allow the people who work for me to be frightened by a bully.

"Well, Miss," Della said, "there's a lady hiding in that old blacksmith shop that was turned into a guesthouse. The Dodges know it. Mr. Dodge takes down her meals on a tray. She's the one you just heard singing."

"Then it's all right, Della," Anne said quietly. "That's their daughter."

"Yes, Miss." The maid gathered up her polishing equipment and went away.

But it's not all right, Anne thought. I don't mind Minna staying here. But why the secrecy? Why is she in hiding? I've waited long enough. It's time to clear things up.

She slipped on her beige topcoat over a powder-blue cardigan and matching skirt. The landscape had changed since her arrival, the trees were stark and bare except for a few tenacious leaves. It was a gray day with mist lying low in the valleys, and the path deep in leaves which were dulled in color and spongy underfoot.

Anne walked swiftly toward the guest cottage. The singing had stopped some time before. As she came in sight of the little stone building she heard voices, and stood quite still, concealed by a hedge.

It was Pedro Brocchi's voice she heard first. He was in the middle of a sentence. ". . . because I can't give you diamonds," he was saying.

"You don't understand," Minna protested.

"You're the one who doesn't understand," Pedro said. "I've told you all the time it's dangerous. You little fool, you can't get away with it."

"Oh, let me alone! Nag, nag, nag all the time."

"I have to warn you, Minna," he said desperately. "I've loved you all my life. I can't just sit back and—"

"Jealous!" she snapped. "You're just jealous. And revengeful. Love me?" she laughed bitterly. "A thief and a blackmailer?"

"I'm only trying to help you—"

"By stealing the money Mrs. Williams intended for me—by threatening—"

"I haven't touched that ten thousand dollars."

"Then why did you take it?"

"To save you from—"

There was a roar of anger. Dodge came plunging around the side of the stone cottage. "I've got you now," he yelled.

From her shelter behind the hedge, Anne peered cautiously toward the cottage. She saw Dodge, lips curled back from his teeth, his bony hands tightening around Pedro's throat. She saw Minna shrinking back into the open doorway.

"I've got you now," Dodge shouted again. He shook the small, slight Pedro like a dog. "You've been trying to see Miss Kendrick." *Shake.* "You followed her through the woods." *Shake.* "You nearly knocked me out when I got hold of you." *Shake.*

Pedro's head bobbed helplessly back and forth.

"What did you want with her?" The butler loosened his grip on the younger man's throat.

"I didn't mean to hurt her," Pedro said hoarsely.

"I don't care whether she's hurt or not," Dodge snarled. "What did you want with her?"

"Just to talk. I swear that's all. Just to talk to her."

"Blackmail again? I suppose you were going to ask Miss Kendrick for money to keep still about the fact she doesn't really have a right to the Williams estate. That it?"

"No, no. You know I wouldn't do that."

"Do I? Why did you climb the ivy to break into Mountain Lodge?"

"I knew Minna was there somewhere. I was looking for her."

"If you ever look for her again," Dodge said, "you'll be sorry you were born. I have half a mind—" His hands clutched again at Pedro's throat.

"No! No!" It was Minna's scream. She ran forward, pulling desperately at her father's hands. "No! Don't hurt him."

"Get away," her father said.

"Let him go!" Minna cried. "Let him go or I'll drop the whole thing. I don't care that much about the money. I—"

Dodge's hands fell to his sides. "But it's yours," he exploded. "It's all—"

"Let him go."

Dodge stood back. "Get out of here," he said to Pedro. "I'm letting you go this time. But never again. Is that clear? Scram!"

Pedro's hands were at his neck, his breath was coming in great broken gusts. He turned to Minna. "I knew you loved me." Before she could speak he turned swiftly and disappeared around the corner of the house.

Dodge took a step toward his daughter, his expression so menacing that, with a little smothered cry, she ran inside the cottage and bolted the door.

Anne, her knees trembling, sank down on the ground and remained where she was until Dodge had gone back to the house. Then at last she retraced her steps. As she went up to the entrance she looked at the massive, formidable door. It seemed to threaten her. From the first it had threatened rather than welcomed her. Even if it is mine, she decided, I won't live at Mountain Lodge. Beautiful, maybe, but not friendly, not home.

Dodge opened the door for her, his ear twitching madly. There was scarcely concealed insolence in his manner. He hovered in the background as Anne made her telephone call but for once she didn't care.

134

"Mr. Cosgrove, this is Anne Kendrick. I'd like to see you at once."

There was a moment's hesitation and then the lawyer said soberly, "As a matter of fact, I was about to call you. A conference seems to be in order."

"I'll be there in thirty minutes," Anne told him.

When she entered his office Cosgrove pushed back his chair and came forward to meet her. His white hair looked as though he had been running his fingers through it. His young face was grave. He did not smile as he welcomed her.

"Sit here, Miss Kendrick," he said in a worried tone. "I think you'll be more comfortable."

When she was seated he looked toward the door and the telephone, as though hoping some interruption would postpone an unpleasant interview. He offered her a cigarette, which she refused, and with her permission lighted one for himself.

"What a girl," he said, trying to strike a light note. "Never smokes. Never drinks. By the way, have you heard anything about your friend Crane?"

"He isn't my friend," Anne said.

"My mistake. You don't need to snap my head off. But you were the one who introduced us. Remember? It got me into a pretty unpleasant spot."

Anne gasped. "But I didn't know—"

"Neither did I. That hasn't kept me from a lot of unpleasant questioning and suspicion. Rumors get around, Miss Kendrick. When a man is running for political office—"

"I'm terribly sorry."

For the first time the lawyer smiled. "When you are in dead earnest those gray-blue eyes of yours turn amethyst. Go ahead, Miss Kendrick. Ladies first. Why did you want to see me?"

"I want you to pension off the Dodges for me," she said. "I won't have them at Mountain Lodge any more. From the moment I entered that house Dodge has been growing worse and worse. He acts as though he owns the place. He frightens and bullies the other servants. He's insolent to me. And Mrs. Dodge is just as bad. She has actually tried to drive me out of the house. They must go and go at once."

Cosgrove turned a pencil around and around in his fingers. At last he said, "Sorry, Miss Kendrick. I'm afraid I can't do that."

"Why not?" Anne demanded.

"The other day I told you there had been some startling new developments. Do you recall that?"

She nodded.

"For your sake I hoped—" Cosgrove broke off. "I might as well tell you the truth—I'm afraid it will be a terrific shock—"

Anne cried, "Anything is better than suspense."

"Well, here it is. The missing will has been found, Miss Kendrick. A later will than the one that made you sole heir. According to the new one, everything goes to Jimmy Williams. That means his widow—Minna Dodge Williams."

As though in a dream Anne heard him say, "You see, Miss Kendrick, I can't order the Dodges to leave Mountain Lodge. As things stand now, they have more right there than you have."

XXIV

"YOU KNOW," Anne surprised herself by saying, "I don't believe it."

"What do you mean?" Cosgrove asked sharply. "I realize this is a big disappointment, Miss Kendrick—"

"No," Anne said slowly. "That isn't it. Of course, it's a shock. I've never been so surprised. But I don't actually mind very much about losing the money."

Seeing Cosgrove's unbelieving smile, she added eagerly, "That's really true. Just because there was so terribly much of it and it came like a thunderbolt from a clear sky—no, more like something in a fairy tale—it never seemed quite real. And it's been mine only a few weeks. Not really time to get used to it. But—"

"Well? If you are questioning the legality—" he began stiffly.

"You see," Anne said, "since I've been up here and learned more about Mrs. Williams, the kind of woman she was, her sense of responsibility to her fortune, I just don't believe she would have left that fortune to her irresponsible stepson. Certainly she would never have been willing to let her property go to the Dodges. She didn't approve of Minna."

As Cosgrove started to speak she went on quickly, "Wait, Mr. Cosgrove. Let me explain. She knew Jimmy was dead. Even if she had made a will in his favor she would have changed it after his death. Especially when she learned that Minna claimed to be his widow."

"Believe me," Cosgrove said, a ring of sincerity in his voice, "I've been as surprised and shocked as you are by all this. I've been investigating thoroughly to make sure no second mistake was possible. There is none. The will making Jimmy Williams sole heir will stand in court."

"Where did you find it?"

"I was going through a miscellaneous bunch of papers the

other day. They were old personal letters Mrs. Williams had kept for sentimental reasons—most of them from your father, by the way. I had never looked through them before. The will was clipped accidentally to one of them. It's the same will I drew for her—as a matter of fact, the only will I knew she had made until the one in your favor was unearthed after her death. Now that I go over that will, Miss Kendrick, I have an uneasy feeling that the signature isn't like the others. I don't say it was forged, but—"

"Why," Anne demanded, "would anyone try to forge a will in my favor? Who would gain by it?"

He shrugged his shoulders.

"Doesn't a signature to a will have to be witnessed?"

"Naturally. The will in your favor was witnessed by a gardener who has since died—and by Griffith Trent."

"And the other will—the later will?"

"Witnessed by the Dodges." Cosgrove got up and walked to the window. He returned to his desk. "Still not satisfied?"

"Something bothers me," Anne admitted. "Since coming up here I've acquired a feeling of responsibility about this estate. Are you sure Minna Dodge ever married Jimmy Williams?"

Cosgrove smiled. "You must think I'm a child at this game, Miss Kendrick. I've been practicing law almost as long as you've been alive. I've had a detective check on the marriage. The records were found in a little town in upper New York State."

"Then why," Anne demanded, "if Minna Dodge is really Mrs. Jimmy Williams, is Pedro Brocchi trying to blackmail her? There must be—"

"What's that?" Cosgrove leaped to his feet, his prominent eyeballs seeming to pop out on his cheeks.

Anne described the conversation she had overhead between Pedro and Minna, and Dodge's quarrel with Pedro.

"Dodge was afraid Pedro would try to tell me something. What? It could only be something about Minna's right to inherit the property. You remember, I told you when they talked in the nurse-companion's room, he said he knew 'all about the mysterious missing will.' "

"And has this fellow Brocchi tried to talk to you?"

Anne shook her head. "Unless that's what he wanted when he followed me from Forest Edge and—" She started to describe his appearance in the back of the car and remembered that Griff had warned her not to speak.

"What became of him?"

"I don't know. He ran before Dodge could get his hands on him. Ugh!" She shivered. "That man is really a bully."

Cosgrove nodded. "I don't like Dodge too much myself.

137

It will be a relief to you to leave Mountain Lodge. When do you expect to go?"

Anne looked at him blankly. "I don't know. I have no plans. This is so—unexpected—so completely new to me—"

He got to his feet. His manner was entirely courteous but there was no question in Anne's mind that he was dismissing her. After all, she was no longer the heir to Mountain Lodge and a great fortune. She was an ex-client, imposing on the time of a busy man.

"If I can help you in any way," Cosgrove said, "don't hesitate to call on me."

"Thank you."

Outside the lawyer's office Anne got in her car and sat for a moment looking through the windshield. Where shall I go, she thought. If I go back to Mountain Lodge—but I don't even belong there. I don't belong anywhere. Someone else has taken over my television program in New York. I haven't even got a job.

Anne Kendrick, you've got to think, she told herself sternly. You need advice. The trustees? But they aren't my trustees any more. If I go back to the house, Dodge will be unbearable. By this time he must know it all belongs to Minna.

But does it? Does it? Some hunch tells me the Dodges are doing something dishonest. Trying to cheat Mrs. Williams. Could be. I don't like to distrust people but—

She remembered Mrs. Dodge's ugly warning that first night, and Dodge saying to Pedro only an hour ago, "I don't care whether she's hurt," and shivered.

It sends ice down my spine to think of it. But what am I going to do?

Griffith Trent! Hadn't he said Mrs. Williams wanted him to help her? With her heart feeling lighter, Anne started the car and drove slowly up the mountain road to Forest Edge. She was so deep in thought she forgot to turn in at the driveway and had to back up.

The smiling maid who admitted her said that Miss Trent was with Miss Sharon but she'd let her know at once. Griff and the big, impressive-looking Congressman whom he had introduced as John Clinton were sitting at a table with papers spread out before them, deep in talk.

They got up as she came in.

"Anne!" Griff exclaimed. "This is a pleasure."

"I'm sorry to interrupt you," Anne said looking at the papers.

Clinton swept them into a briefcase. "We had finished," he said. "We were just talking." He started for the door.

"Don't go," Anne said. "I've got a—a sort of problem—and I need all the advice I can get."

Griff gave her a quick look. Clinton came back. "You shall have all the wisdom I'm capable of."

His face lighted up as Rissa came into the room. She wore a tan skirt with a soft pink blouse, there was a deeper color and warmth in her face than Anne had ever seen there, her eyes were soft and shining.

"Hello, Anne! How nice of you to come."

"Sit down, Rissa," Griff said quietly. "I think Anne has something to tell us."

Anne drew a long, unsteady breath. "That's putting it mildly. I've come to throw a bombshell."

Before she could go on the maid appeared at the door. "Mrs. Mason," she announced.

Zoe Mason, wearing a black crepe dress, hatless, a white wool coat making her dark hair dramatic, came in smiling. Her smile faded as she saw Anne.

"Hello, Rissa. Griff, darling! Mr. Clinton." She added coolly, "How are you, Miss Kendrick? Getting to be quite neighborly. I always seem to find you here."

"Not half neighborly enough to suit us," Rissa declared.

"You said it," put in Griff.

"If I am interrupting anything—" Zoe began.

"It's no secret," Anne said. "Everyone will know about it sooner or later."

"Go ahead," Griff told her. "We're all ears."

"I called Mr. Cosgrove a little while ago and asked him to see me at once. I—I wanted to pension off the Dodges and get rid of them."

"And high time too," Rissa put in.

"When I saw him," Anne went on, "he said he couldn't do it. He said I don't own Mountain Lodge."

"What!"

"He has found the missing will, a later one than the one that made me the heir. Everything goes to Jimmy Williams —or rather to Minna."

There was a moment of stunned silence and then Rissa cried, "No! No! I don't believe it. Aunt Mayme would never in this world—why, John—"

Even in her stunned condition, Anne realized that it was to John Clinton that Rissa turned, not to her brother. She looked at Griff. To her amazement she saw there was a look of satisfaction on his face.

"So that's it!" he exclaimed. "Well, I'll be—so that's it!"

The conversation flowed on around Anne, who curled up on a corner of the deep couch, listening without trying to take any part in it. Rissa and John did most of the talking. Griff, after his first, "So that's it!" was silent, deep in thought. Zoe's eyes moved from his face to Anne's and back again, with the regularity of a windshield wiper.

The talk finally ended with Griff saying, "All of you are too worked up over this thing."

"Worked up!" Rissa exclaimed indignantly. "Really, Griff. You'd think nothing had happened. We can't let the Dodges get away with this."

"I'll take it up with Cosgrove," Griff said. "And now, if you'll excuse me, I have some telephone calls to make."

Perhaps he made the calls but it was not from Forest Edge. A few minutes after he left them Anne saw his car streak away from the house.

At Rissa's insistence Anne agreed to stay for dinner. Zoe, who made it clear that she would outstay Anne if it took all night, received a cooler invitation and accepted quickly.

It was in a brief interlude before dinner when they chanced to be left alone that Anne had her curious and fateful talk with Zoe.

Standing framed against the long drapes at the French windows, Zoe, in her exquisitely fitting black dress, looked like a high-fashion model. The same perfection of detail, the same slightly dehumanized loveliness.

"I'm afraid," she said, "Griff is riding for a fall."

"What do you mean?" Anne asked.

Zoe laughed. "My dear, you simply can't be so blind you don't see what you are doing."

"I don't understand."

The arched eyebrows rose still higher in polite disbelief. "Well, if that's the way you want it— No! I can't keep still and see Griff destroy his career."

Anne gasped. "Destroy his career!"

Zoe looked around to make sure they were alone. "Figure it out for yourself. *Someone*—" and her eyes met Anne's in a direct accusation—"has been busy circulating the idea that Mayme Williams left you a husband and that the man is Griff Trent."

Anne made no reply although the color deepened in her face.

"This isn't New York, you know," Zoe went on. "Up here we like men who make their own way. If Griff's constituents get the idea he's having any part in a matrimonial deal in order to get a share in the Williams money, they're going to be disgusted with him."

"But it's not true," Anne cried. "It's not true."

Zoe studied her face for a moment. "I hope not. But one thing is sure—if Griff goes tearing off to Cosgrove, demanding that you get the money—especially if there is some hocus-pocus about the will—the fat will be in the fire."

140

She broke off and turned with a smile to greet Griff as he came into the room. She linked her arm with his and strolled away with him, saying, "Darling, I'm dying to hear how the campaign is progressing. When do you make your next speech?"

What did she mean—some hocus-pocus about the will? Does Zoe think I had something to do with it? She is certainly staking her claim to Griff. She's done that since the first moment I saw her. But is it true—will it destroy Griff's career if he helps me now?

All through dinner Anne was very silent, speaking only when it was necessary. After dinner she apologized.

"There has been so much strain today I think I'll go back early and get some rest."

"I'll drive for you," Griff said, and Anne saw Zoe's jaw set.

They rode in silence until they came to the side road where Griff had stopped once before. He switched off the motor and turned to face her.

"Anne," he said quietly, "I sent you some roses a few days ago."

"Wonderful roses," she said. "Didn't you get my note of thanks?"

"There was a message with the roses. Did you read it?"

She was silent.

"Perhaps you've forgotten." In the dark Anne could hear him laughing softly. "I'll remind you. The note said, *Perhaps Mayme Williams did leave you a husband.*"

Her heart raced. Oh, Griff, she thought. Oh, Griff!

His arms drew her to him, warm and gentle and strong. He pressed his cheek against hers. "Anne," he whispered, "I love you very much. I think I've been in love with you for two years. Could you—"

For a moment the sweetness of it was almost all that Anne could bear. Then she remembered Zoe's words. It will destroy Griff's career if he marries me. Everyone will think it's the money, that he's the fiancé I invented to get rid of Ned Crane.

Griff leaned over and kissed her on the mouth.

Anne's hands pressed against him. "No, Griff," she said. "No, let me go! Please."

He released her at once. "What is it, Anne? Can't you learn to love me?"

I don't need to try, she thought. Aloud she said, "It's no use. I'm sorry."

"Can you tell me why?"

For a moment the temptation was strong to tell him what Zoe had said. But suppose he made the sacrifice—suppose he said his career did not matter? His country needed him, she had no right to destroy his usefulness.

"I'm sorry," she said again.

Griff started the motor. He did not speak until they reached Mountain Lodge. As he helped her out of the car he smiled.

"Don't worry about it," he said gently. "I should have known that I wouldn't have a chance. But remember that I'm still around if you need me."

XXV

THE LOW sobbing went on and on. Stop it, Anne ordered herself, but she could not stop.

You ought to be satisfied, she thought. You wanted to make Griff Trent fall for you and then give him a brush-off he'd never forget. Well, you've done it. Only it hasn't worked out the way you expected. You're the one who's been hurt.

It's all my own fault. If I hadn't invented that crazy story of Mrs. Williams leaving me a husband this wouldn't have happened. I could have married Griff. But now everyone would believe it was nothing but a marriage for money. I can't hurt Griff and his career like that.

She tossed restlessly. My last night at Mountain Lodge. How strange this has been. The whole thing was a dream—the house, the fortune, Griff—and now the fairy tale is over and I am creeping home at midnight when the magic is over.

This is like my first night at Mountain Lodge. I can't sleep because I'm afraid. But why should I be afraid now? I know who tried to drive me away—the Dodges. There's no mystery any more. There's nothing to be afraid of any more. Tomorrow it will all be theirs. Tomorrow I'll be gone.

Queer—I feel as though the whole house were awake with me. You're letting your imagination run wild, Anne. But I *do* hear things—whispers, people moving unseen in the dark, footsteps.

She sat up in bed, her heart racing, staring into the dark. It's *not* my imagination. Something is going on in this house. Something evil.

From the beginning her fears had centered in the nurse-companion's suite. She stretched out her hand and pressed the button. In a moment it glowed red. She held her breath, listening at the grating.

Nothing—of course there was nothing. Why should there be anything? Someone breathing? No, it was her own quick-drawn breath. She held it for a moment but the sound of even breathing went on. Someone else then! Someone in the nurse-companion's suite.

142

She relaxed. Of course, it must be Minna. The Dodges couldn't wait to take over the house, couldn't wait for her to give up ownership officially. They had moved Minna out of the guest cottage and back into the house.

Anne lay down again and closed her eyes but she could not sleep. Unexpectedly a phrase leaped into her mind, a phrase Zoe Mason had used that afternoon—"If there is some hocus-pocus about the will . . ."

Some hocus-pocus. And Gaston Cosgrove had said the signature looked wrong to him. Anne frowned into the dark. What did they mean? The lawyer had never seen the will that made Anne heir until after Mrs. Williams's death. He had never heard of Anne's existence. And the signature looked wrong. And the only living witness was Griffith Trent!

Steady, Anne, she told herself. You've got to face it. Griff had told her he had watched her for two years at Mrs. Williams's request but no one—not even Rissa—had known that. They were never to know. He had made her promise. Why? *Why?*

Griff had said Mrs. Williams backed him for Congress. Cosgrove had made the same claim for himself. Which one —she forced herself to face the truth—which one was lying?

Which one—all right, Anne, if you are so anxious to be businesslike, start now—which one profited? Not Cosgrove. His position remained the same, no matter who inherited. But Griff—if he married Anne—

No! Anne cried silently in her heart. I can't believe it. I don't believe it. I won't believe it. Not Griff. A fortune hunter like Ned Crane. No, a thousand times no.

There was a sound of footsteps on the stairs. Minna? But the quiet, unhurried breathing still came through the grating. Was it Dodge? There was a crisp assurance about the footsteps. Who had said that character could be told by footsteps? Mrs. Williams, who had listened to people walking up and down those uncovered marble stairs. Somewhere a door closed softly.

More footsteps! Determined steps. The kind that would not easily be stopped. Anne could imagine those ruthless feet treading on anything that got in their way. They broke off suddenly.

Who are these people? What are they doing here? I'm afraid. Oh, Griff, you said you'd be around when I needed you. I need you now.

And then, unbelievably, horribly, Anne heard Griff's voice through the grating.

"I tell you," he said in a voice of command Anne had never before heard him use, "to do as I say. Get her away tonight—"

"But," began another voice, Pedro Brocchi's voice.

"—if you have to kidnap her," Griff concluded.

Oh, no, Anne thought, too heartsick to be frightened. No, this can't be happening.

Then her chin went up, there was courage and decision in her face. She turned on the light, got out of bed and dressed hastily in dark slacks and a navy-blue sweater, moccasins on her feet. She tied a navy-blue scarf over her bright hair, pulled on her dark cape and checked her shoulder bag to make sure she had money.

She switched off the light and made her way noiselessly to the door and pushed back the bolt. She put her hands on the doorknob.

An icy chill ran down her spine. Under her fingers she felt the knob turn.

She reached for the bolt but it was too late. The door was slowly moving inward. Step by step Anne retreated in the dark. "—if you have to kidnap her," Griff had said.

She was against the wall now, she could retreat no farther. The door opened wide. Someone was inside the room with her.

Anne held her breath and for a moment there was no sound at all. The intruder was still, listening to see whether she was awake.

Then there was a movement, so light she would never have heard it if every sense had not been alert. A shadowy figure was going slowly toward the bed.

Anne kept one hand against the wall, ears straining, lips parted. Carefully she timed her own steps, moving each time the shadow moved. As it took one step toward the bed she took one toward the door. Another. Another. She could feel a draft on her ankles now from the open door.

There was a whisper of cloth brushing against cloth. The intruder had reached the bed—was groping—

With a whisk of movement Anne was outside the door, running toward the marble stairs. No time for silence now. She raced down them, running toward the front door. If only the chain had been left off. If only—

Someone was pounding down the stairs after her. She was halfway across the hallway when she saw someone duck behind one of the huge Chinese vases that stood on either side of the entrance. She was hemmed in.

With a sob in her throat Anne wheeled, running toward the entertainment suite. She opened the first door, dashed inside and closed the door behind her.

In the dark she groped her way across the room toward the long windows that opened out on the terrace.

There was a muffled shout in the hall. Men were fighting. More feet clattering down the marble stairs. Had the whole world gone mad?

The door to the hall opened and closed again. Someone was in the room with her. Someone standing very still.

Outside there was a shout. "He got away!"

"How?"

"I don't know. Not through the front door. I've never left it."

Somewhere in the room a floor board creaked. Anne ducked behind a chair. Another board creaked—closer to her.

I know now how a deer feels when it is stalked, Anne thought. On hands and knees she crawled backwards, still sheltered by the broad back of the winged chair. Something brushed her ankles and she smothered a scream. It was the drapes. She had reached the windows.

Men were running now. "I've got the back covered . . . Turn on the light . . . Route out the servants . . ."

Anne opened her mouth to scream for help and pressed her hand over her mouth. Friend or foe? Which was which?

". . . if you have to kidnap her . . . if you have to kidnap her." The words repeated themselves dully in her mind.

She pulled herself slowly to her feet, drawing the drapes in front of her. She groped for the catch of the window. Would the click betray her presence? Could she get the window open before she was caught?

The door opened with a bang and the lights went on. There was a shout and then the sound of fighting, men stumbling, bumping into furniture, blows, grunts, heavy breathing.

People were running now. Cautiously, Anne opened a crack in the draperies. The room seemed to be full of people. But she had eyes only for the two who struggled in the midst of the shambles of furniture. Gaston Cosgrove had caught Griffith Trent with a low tackle and, while Anne watched, Griff fell heavily to the floor.

Not Griff, Anne thought. Not Griff. The pain of her disillusionment was unbearable. Her knees crumpled and she fell forward, mercifully unconscious.

The next hour was a period of delirium. Later it was hard to know what had been real, what had been mad pictures of a feverish mind.

There was a time of lights and loud voices and a tangle of men scuffling. There were the arms that lifted her from the floor and laid her on the chesterfield. There were the faces she expected to see: Dodge and his wife, Cosgrove and Griff. There were faces she did not expect to see: Joe Bennet in his Marine uniform, red hair standing up wildly, Minna Dodge crying on the shoulder of Pedro Brocchi.

145

There was darkness again and fever and a throbbing head. There was a rocking movement, the sound of a motor. I'm being taken somewhere, Anne thought dimly. I'm being kidnaped.

XXVI

IT WAS the sun that awakened Anne. She moved her head restlessly to avoid the glare and then her eyes opened. She was in a strange room, sun-flooded, with powder-blue walls and drapes the color of golden dandelions at the casement windows.

The tantalizing scent of coffee and bacon made her turn her head.

"The Sleeping Beauty awakens," said a laughing voice.

"Rissa!" Anne exclaimed in bewilderment.

Clarissa Trent stood beside the bed, holding a breakfast tray. "Sit up and eat your breakfast," she said.

"But where—why—what—"

"You eat and I talk. If you don't eat I won't talk. Those were my orders."

"Doctor's orders?" Anne said, trying to speak lightly, as memories began to flood her mind.

"Griff's orders." Rissa, wearing a floor-length white housecoat that buttoned up to the throat, smiled down at Anne as she poured the coffee.

"Now then," she began, pulling a low rocker close to the bed. "I'll answer some of the questions that must be driving you crazy. You look a lot better this morning. When Griff brought you here to Forest Edge last night and carried you into the house, unconscious, I was worried sick. We called a doctor but he said it was only shock and exhaustion. Nothing that plenty of rest won't cure."

Anne blinked at her in bewilderment. She sipped the coffee, discovered that she was ravenously hungry and began to eat.

"You probably don't remember much of what happened," Rissa went on. "Before I tell you the whole story, though, I want to explain that your troubles are over; there's nothing else to bother you. Dodge is under arrest and so is Gaston Cosgrove."

"What!"

"Look out!" Rissa jumped up and rescued the silver coffeepot which was rocking precariously on the tray. "Yes, Gaston Cosgrove. Don't give any more of those wild leaps, Anne, or you will drown in hot coffee."

"Go on talking," Anne wailed, "before I go out of my mind. Gaston Cosgrove!"

Rissa laughed and then grew sober again. "I know. I was as flabbergasted as you are when I heard the story. Griff worked it out."

"Tell me—" Anne begged.

"Only if you keep on eating. You must have food."

"Please—"

"All right. It goes back to the fact that Gaston Cosgrove is a very ambitious man. When he landed the management of Aunt Mayme's estate and realized what an eccentric woman she was, he began to scheme to get her fortune into his own hands."

"I remember Joe Bennet telling me he was tricky in his relations with human beings."

"He was all of that," Rissa agreed. "Well, he soon discovered that while she was eccentric she was also a shrewd business woman and he could not get by with any trickery while she lived. So he began to plan to get his hands on her money after her death. He knew he would never persuade her to make a will in his favor. But suppose a will should be found leaving the money to Jimmy. The estate would go to Jimmy's heirs.

"That is when the idea grew of faking a marriage between Jimmy and Minna Dodge. As a kid, Jimmy had been attracted to her. The Dodges had had her around the house to catch his eye but Mrs. Williams had sent the girl away.

"Cosgrove knew the Dodges through and through. They would do anything for money. So they worked on Minna. She didn't want to do it but it was hard to hold out when her own father and mother hammered at her day and night."

"I always felt sorry for Minna," Anne said.

"She and Pedro Brocchi had been girl-and-boy sweethearts. He loved her and I think she really loved him. But Cosgrove gave her presents of diamonds, telling her they were nothing compared to what she would get as her share if she went through with his plans. The diamonds turned the trick."

Rissa smiled. "You look better already. There's some color in your cheeks. I'll give you time for your bath and when you are dressed we'll continue this discussion downstairs. There are some other people who want to sit in on this. Among them Joe Bennet."

"Joe! Then it wasn't a dream that I saw him last night."

"From all I can make out, it was far from a dream. Griff seems to have had people stationed all over that house last night. Joe was due for his first leave and he tells me he had a post guarding the front door. Pedro was on guard in the nurse-companion's suite."

147

At the doorway Rissa paused. "Oh, by the way, your maid brought over some clothes for you this morning."

When she had finished dressing, Anne looked at herself in the mirror. The emerald-green Shantung dress with the huge tie of black velvet under her chin made her hair look like honey. Her eyes were two amethysts in her flushed face. Slowly the radiance died out of it. True, Griff had not been guilty of an attempt to kidnap her as she had thought for a black moment, but he was separated from her as much as before. She still could not marry him without destroying his career.

So it was a sober Anne who went down the spiral staircase into the room below.

Sharon came running to meet her. "Can you forgive me for being such a dope?"

Anne laughed and kissed her. "There's nothing to forgive," she declared.

Joe Bennet, erect and military in his trim uniform, shook hands heartily. Griff looked at her swiftly to make sure she was all right, that she had recovered, and his eyes glowed with pleasure. Anne gave him a tremulous smile as she sat down.

"You take up the story, Griff," Rissa said. "After all, you're the one who worked it out."

Griff shook his head. "The real credit goes to Pedro," he said. "The night we had that long talk at Parson Savage's, he told me the whole thing. The poor guy was almost frantic trying to prevent Minna's committing a criminal action. He was tickled to death to have a chance to get it off his chest.

"This is the story Pedro told me that night. Cosgrove by bribery got the marriage entered in the records of a small town, forged a marriage certificate and a will making Jimmy the sole heir. All he had to do then was to wait for Aunt Mayme to die, and any sudden shock might accomplish that.

"It was Dodge who precipitated the trouble. Mrs. Williams · might live for years. Minna had some diamonds but he— Dodge—wasn't getting anything out of it at all. What he wanted was cash in hand. So, without telling Cosgrove, he had Minna come up to Mountain Lodge, tell Aunt Mayme she was Jimmy's widow, produce the marriage certificate and ask for Jimmy's insurance money.

"Aunt Mayme, as we know, drew the money out of the bank. But Pedro, who had been crazy with jealousy since Minna started wearing diamonds, had followed her to Mountain Lodge and overheard that conversation, crouching under the open window of the game room. He saw through the whole plot in a flash because he knew Minna had never married Jimmy."

"Pedro always was one smart *hombre*," Joe commented. "Or, as he would say, 'a smart cooky.'"

"It was that 'smart cooky' expression of his," Griff went on, "that caused the death of poor Old Soc, the gray parrot. Pedro didn't want Minna to take the ten thousand dollars from Mrs. Williams under false pretenses. If she were ever found out, she'd be guilty of felony. So Pedro climbed up the vine, to avoid Dodge, got into the game room, and told Mrs. Williams the truth: that Cosgrove and Dodge were conspiring to get her money through a faked will and a bogus marriage.

"Mrs. Williams, realizing Pedro's mad jealousy, did not believe him, but she decided to have Cosgrove hire a detective to check on Jimmy's marriage. She believed the lawyer was honest but she was not sure about Dodge. She telephoned Cosgrove and he came to see her. You can imagine his shock when he realized she knew the truth about his plot. But the worst shock was hers when she looked at him and saw he was afraid—and realized the story was true."

"Poor Aunt Mayme," Rissa said softly.

"Yes," Griff agreed soberly, "poor Aunt Mayme. That shock killed her. At state-police headquarters last night Cosgrove admitted that she looked at him and fell back dead. He was in a panic. He knew she had made a memorandum because she referred to it during the interview but he couldn't look for it—That, by the way," he told Anne, "explains why they were so frantic to get at Aunt Mayme's clothes closet. They knew the note was there but not how it was phrased. They were afraid it would reveal the whole plot.

"Then Old Soc began to squawk, 'Cosgrove is a smart cooky,' and Cosgrove lost his head. He took the parrot with him and got out of there."

Griff paused to fill and light his pipe. "Well," he went on, "Cosgrove was all ready to go into action and produce the will he had forged but, before he could do it, the safety deposit box was opened and there was Mayme Williams's own will, leaving everything to a girl he had never heard of —Anne Kendrick. It must have been the biggest shock Cosgrove ever had."

"It was the biggest shock I ever had," Anne admitted. Something clicked in her mind. That story Cosgrove had told her of Griff refusing to marry her was a lie, invented on the spur of the moment, to make Anne dislike Griff. How close he had come to succeeding!

"The papers played the story up in a big way. Cosgrove didn't dare spring his own faked will because Pedro Brocchi had gone to see him and threatened him with exposure if he made a move. Before he could deal with Anne he had to deal with Pedro.

"Cosgrove offered Pedro a percentage if he would keep still and Pedro pretended to be interested. He believed if he could just make Minna see what she was doing she would give it up. He told me, 'I love her, Mr. Trent. She's never had a chance. At heart she's all right. I'd stake my life on that.'"

"I guess I don't need to be sorry for any woman who is loved like that," Anne said.

Griff looked at her soberly for a moment and she could feel her cheeks flaming.

"Cosgrove thought, mistakenly, he had Pedro under control so he began to wonder about Anne. He got hold of a confidence man named Ned Crane—" Sharon moved closer to her aunt, who put an arm around her comfortingly—"and had him look her up."

"But how did Cosgrove get in touch with Ned Crane?" Rissa asked. "Such an extraordinary coincidence."

Griff looked at her quickly but he saw there was nothing to worry about. His sister was puzzled, but nothing that concerned Crane would ever hurt her again.

"The next part of this story," he said, "comes from the FBI in New York. Crane was terrified when they arrested him. He's a slick crook but he wasn't prepared to fight the U.S. Government. All he wanted was to get clear and throw the blame on Cosgrove.

"It seems Crane and Cosgrove have known each other for a long time. It was Cosgrove who arranged to have Crane meet Rissa a few years ago, with the agreement that if Crane married her, Cosgrove would get twenty-five thousand dollars —of Rissa's money, of course."

John Clinton growled something under his breath, his fist clenched.

"Well, Cosgrove wrote to Crane and told him to look Anne Kendrick over and report on the kind of person she was. Crane had a better idea. He thought it would be smart to marry her and get a nice share of the Williams money."

"I'm beginning to hate that money!" Anne exclaimed.

"Anyway, Crane was scheduled to come up here, accidentally meet some people and present them to Cosgrove. Crane did not know they were Communists. Cosgrove did, but he desperately needed cash for his political campaign and he thought he would be covered in this way.

"Tim Marston's photographic eye stopped that. Meanwhile the parrot had escaped, a farmer found it and Crane, eavesdropping at the club after I'd thrown him over a wall, learned where it was. He wanted a hold over Cosgrove and took the parrot to Pedro. Later Cosgrove found it there and killed it."

There was a little pause. Then Griff looked at Anne and smiled faintly. "Cosgrove has been having a bad time of it. You appeared on the scene, Dodge wanted more than his share and so did Crane, Pedro threatened exposure and worked on Minna constantly to give up the whole idea. Then you demanded that Dodge be fired. Cosgrove did not dare do that so he made the plunge and produced the 'later will.' We've been waiting for him to make a break. Last night I smuggled Pedro and Joe into your house. I told Pedro to get Minna away and marry her if he had to kidnap her to do it."

"Who—" Anne's throat closed. "Who stalked me through the house?"

"Cosgrove."

"Why?"

"He was looking for Pedro. He knew that Pedro would always be a potential danger to him. I had a long talk with Minna last evening and she came over to our side. She told Cosgrove Pedro was hiding up there, so that he would make an attempt to get him." Seeing how white she was Griff said quickly, "It's all over now. You're safe, Anne."

* * *

As they climbed the steps at Mountain Lodge Anne looked up at the massive, formidable front door.

"From the very first time I saw it," she said, "I thought it was threatening. I don't believe I can ever live at Mountain Lodge, Griff. Perhaps it can be used as a convalescent home for veterans."

"That's a swell idea," he said enthusiastically.

Della, the blond parlormaid, opened the door for them, her eyes wide with excitement. "I'm glad you're home, Miss," she said fervently. "No one knows what to do. There's no one to give orders. Mr. Dodge was taken away by the police and Mrs. Dodge is locked in her room, screaming and carrying on."

"Everything is under control now, Della," Griff told her cheerfully. "Tell the staff that Miss Kendrick is at the wheel now."

"Yes, sir. They'll be mighty glad to hear it."

Anne half expected Griff to say good-by at the door but he followed her purposefully up to the game room. She shivered as she looked around her.

Griff's hand touched her shoulder. "It's all over now," he reminded her.

"I know. I'm being silly."

151

"You've been extremely brave," he said. "Anne—"

Her breath was coming quickly. She did not have the strength to fight against him now.

"Griff," she interrupted, "what shall I do about Mrs. Dodge?"

"Pension her off. Let her go at once."

"What will happen to Minna?"

There was a warm smile on his fine face that curved his lips and lighted his eyes. "Minna," he said, "is going to marry Pedro. I imagine that's what Mrs. Dodge has been 'carrying on' about. Oh, that reminds me, I have something for you."

"For me?"

Griff pulled out of his pocket a thick package of new hundred-dollar bills. "Ten thousand dollars," he said, "with the compliments of Pedro Brocchi."

For a long moment Anne held the package in her hand, flipping the bills back and forth.

"I've never seen so much money," she said at last. "To think it could cause such awful trouble. Griff, I don't want this." She met his eyes in a troubled flash.

"What do you want to do with it?"

"I want to give it to Pedro and Minna for a wedding present. Oh, and I must remember to send the Wingates five hundred dollars for putting us on the track of poor Old Soc."

Griff's arms went around her and he kissed her. "That's what I hoped you would do. You never disappoint me." He went on in a determined tone, "Anne—"

"Griff," she interrupted, again breathlessly, "what—what will happen to Mr. Cosgrove's candidacy?"

Griff laughed. "I think we've heard the last of it. Anne—" this time his hands were on her shoulders, he turned her so that she had to meet his eyes—"it's time I ask some questions and I want the truth from you." As she tried to get away his hands held hers firmly but gently.

"Do you love me?"

That's not a fair question, she thought. It's not fair.

"I told you I couldn't marry you," she said.

"That's not what I asked you."

She was silent. His arms closed around her.

"Let me go, Griff. Please let me go."

"I want to tell you first about a girl I know, a girl I've known for two years, always at a distance, unable to talk to her. A girl who took trouble and disappointment in her stride and didn't complain, a girl who brought sunshine and laughter with her, a girl—" he cleared his throat—"a girl I've been in love with for a long time, a girl I'll love all my life—"

"Griff," she said in a choked voice, her cheek pressed against his jacket, "you aren't thinking of your career."

"The deuce I'm not!" He laughed down at her. "You don't know how crafty I am. I have my eyes on a girl who will share my career, work at it, make it worth-while for me— Anne!" His eyes narrowed. "My career—has Zoe Mason been spreading any of her poison?"

"Well—"

"So that's it! Maybe you'd like to know Zoe left for Florida this morning. My career is what you and I make it. Mayme Williams did talk to me about you. She hoped perhaps some day—she left you a husband if you'll take him—"

"Griff!"

At length he released her. "My vacation is about over. When will you marry me and come down to brighten my house in Washington?"

"Soon," she promised, "very soon. But there's plenty of time, Griff. All the rest of our lives."

SPECIAL OFFER: If you enjoyed this book and would like to have our catalog of over 1,400 other Bantam titles, just send your name and address and 50¢ (to help defray postage and handling costs) to: Catalog Department, Bantam Books, Inc., 414 East Golf Rd., Des Plaines, Ill. 60016.

EMILIE LORING

Women of all ages are falling under the enchanting spell Emilie Loring weaves in her beautiful novels. Once you have finished one book by her, you will surely want to read them all.

☐	12409	HOW CAN THE HEART FORGET	$1.50
☐	12948	RAINBOW AT DUSK	$1.75
☐	12949	WHEN HEARTS ARE LIGHT AGAIN	$1.75
☐	12947	WHERE BEAUTY DWELLS	$1.75
☐	12946	FOLLOW YOUR HEART	$1.75
☐	13450	FOR ALL YOUR LIFE	$1.75
☐	12945	ACROSS THE YEARS	$1.75
☐	12944	GIVE ME ONE SUMMER	$1.75

Buy them at your local bookstore or use this handy coupon for ordering:

Bantam Books, Inc., Dept. EL, 414 East Golf Road, Des Plaines, Ill. 60016

Please send me the books I have checked above. I am enclosing $_____ (please add $1.00 to cover postage and handling). Send check or money order —no cash or C.O.D.'s please.

Mr/Mrs/Miss_____

Address_____

City_____State/Zip_____

EL—3/80

Please allow four to six weeks for delivery. This offer expires 9/80.